disquiet

JULIA LEIGH

disquiet

PENGUIN BOOKS

PENGUIN BOOKS

Published by the Penguin Group

Penguin Group (USA) Inc., 375 Hudson Street, New York, New York 10014, U.S.A.

Penguin Group (Canada), 90 Eglinton Avenue East, Suite 700, Toronto,

Ontario, Canada M4P 2Y3 (a division of Pearson Penguin Canada Inc.)

Penguin Books Ltd, 80 Strand, London WC2R 0RL, England

Penguin Ireland, 25 St Stephen's Green, Dublin 2, Ireland (a division of Penguin Books Ltd)

Penguin Group (Australia), 250 Camberwell Road, Camberwell,

Victoria 3124, Australia (a division of Pearson Australia Group Pty Ltd)

Penguin Books India Pvt Ltd, 11 Community Centre, Panchsheel Park, New Delhi – 110 017, India

Penguin Group (NZ), 67 Apollo Drive, Rosedale, North Shore 0632,

New Zealand (a division of Pearson New Zealand Ltd)

Penguin Books (South Africa) (Pty) Ltd, 24 Sturdee Avenue,

Rosebank, Johannesburg 2196, South Africa

Penguin Books Ltd, Registered Offices:
80 Strand, London WC2R 0RL, England

First published in Australia by Hamish Hamilton, an imprint of Penguin Group (Australia) 2008
Published in Penguin Books (USA) 2008

1   3   5   7   9   10   8   6   4   2

PUBLISHER'S NOTE

This is a work of fiction. Names, characters, places, and incidents are either the product
of the author's imagination or are used fictitiously, and any resemblance to actual persons,
living or dead, business establishments, events, or locales is entirely coincidental.

LIBRARY OF CONGRESS CATALOGING IN PUBLICATION DATA
Leigh, Julia, 1970–
Disquiet / Julia Leigh.
p.   cm.
ISBN 978-0-14-311350-8
1. Family reunions—Fiction   2. Abused wives—Fiction.   3. Bereavement—Psychological aspects—
Fiction.   4. Children—Death—Fiction.   5. France—Fiction.   6. Domestic fiction.   I. Title.
PR9619.3.L4417D57   2008
823'.914—dc22   2008012420

Printed in the United States of America
Design by Marina Messiha

Avec ma main brûlée, j'écris sur la nature du feu.

With my burnt hand I write about the nature of fire.
Ingeborg Bachmann, *Malina*, after Gustav Flaubert,
Letter to Louise Colet, 6 July 1852.

They stood before the great gateway, all around an empty and open countryside, ugly countryside, flat mud-ploughed fields. On that morning the sky was balm, a pale and whitish blue. The woman was dressed in a tweed pencil skirt, a grey silk blouse and her dark hair was pulled back into a loose chignon, the way her mother once used to wear it. Her right arm was broken and she'd rested it in a silk-scarf sling which co-ordinated unobtrusively with her blouse. By her feet, a suitcase. The children – the boy was nine, the girl was six and carrying her favourite doll – were saddled with backpacks and they each guarded a small suitcase of their own. The woman stepped forward and went right up to the gate – iron-spiked, imposing – looking for the lock. Instead she found the surveillance system, a palmpad, and she rested her palm on this electronic pad for a long moment until she was defeated. Unfazed, she returned to collect her suitcase and, without a backward glance at the children, turned off the driveway onto the grassy verge.

After a while they decided to follow. First the boy, then the girl. They lumbered in single file alongside the stone wall that bordered the vast estate until the woman reached a spot which looked familiar; she had recognised an ancient oak over the bristling glass-topped wall. A sweet-smelling vine covered this section of the wall and, hooking the handle of her suitcase awkwardly over her cast, she trailed her left hand through the greenery, seeking out the stone behind it. Until she found – the door. She tore at the vine and when the children joined her they watched this motherly performance with the same impassive look on their faces that they usually had when they watched TV. But the boy soon came to help and eventually they uncovered the small wooden entrance. She still had her key and – holding the slender precious thing in her left-hand mitt, the 'sinister hand' – she fitted it to the lock. At first she turned it in the wrong direction but then, click, they heard the tumbler fall. The door didn't open, would not open: she tried, it stayed shut. She pressed her full bodyweight against it, leant into it with her shoulder, but it refused to budge. She stood there for a long while with her forehead resting against the door, as if by dint of will it somehow, if only, would melt away and allow them to pass.

The boy had a go. He planted himself on the ground and kicked at the door. He kicked and kicked, first a hard low kick and then a one-two kung-fu kick. He took a few steps back and, like a high-jumper, standing on the balls of his feet, gathering concentration, he readied for a run-up: he launched himself against the door. At the point of impact there came a dull thud. He did this again; he made himself brutal. And again. Over and over, uncomplaining. He picked himself up, wincing, and walked back to his starting position, lifted his heels, ran at the door. But the door was oak and he was boy; his shirt was torn and bloodied. He snuck a glance at the woman and with a slow blink she encouraged him to continue. In the end he forced an opening.

The woman was first through the breach, snagging and ripping her stockings. The boy helped his sister across and then, piece by piece, passed the luggage over. He took a quick look around to make sure no-one had been watching and closed the door behind him.

———

Once inside they dragged their suitcases through lawn that grew thick and soft. In the distance a squad of four men, gardeners in uniform, were scooping leaves out of a stone-sculpted fountain. As the trio drew close one of these gardeners, a longtimer, struggled to his feet and waved in greeting. The woman returned his wave but did not deviate from her course. They followed the long line of yews clipped into fantastic shapes, into top hats and ice-cream cones and barbells. Another gardener, riding on a mower, swerved to give them berth. They avoided the rose garden and instead cut into the pebbled allée which was lined with elms whose twigs had not yet sprouted their leaves, so that it was apparent a tree actually grew, that a twig had worked its way out of a branch, that an elm did not arrive in the world elm-shaped. The girl declined to leave the lawn, would not put a foot onto the allée, until her brother opened her suitcase and from it removed the tiny exoskeleton of a pram. She settled her doll into the pram and, reassured, proceeded on, managing to push the pram and pull her suitcase at one and the same time.

The stone stairs leading to the château were wide and shallow and worn like soap. The woman took hold of the doorknocker – it was a large bronze ring running through the nose of a great bronze bull – and weighed it in her hand. Knocked. They waited patiently, and their kind of patience was born more from exhaustion, from abandoning any expectation of easy gratification, than from gracious goodwill. She reached out to ruffle the boy's hair, to give them both some courage. Knock-knock. An old woman answered. She was wearing her perennial uniform, a black dress and white apron, and her hair, grey now, was curled in a tidy bun. They stared at one another without speaking and between them passed an understanding of the unsung miracle of the door – one moment a person wasn't there, and the next moment . . . there. Peering inside, the children spied the entrance hall; it was austere and immense, the wood-panelled walls were painted palest dove-grey. High ceilings lent it the authority of a church or a courthouse although this authority was undermined by brightly coloured helium balloons weighted down in vases and tied along the banisters of the grand central staircase.

'Hello Ida,' said the woman calmly. 'It's me.'

'Hello Olivia.'

'May I introduce the children?'

Each child gave a limp wave. Ida noted the boy's bloodied shoulder, his torn shirt and trousers, but held her tongue. She bent down and twinkled her fingers in greeting, ushered them inside.

Grandmother crowned the staircase. She was impeccably dressed in a matching bouclé jacket and skirt, a faultless string of pearls. A sceptral silver-topped walking-stick rested by her side. Though small and frail, the impression she gave was one of dignified resignation.

'Hello Mother.'

'Hello Olivia.'

The woman climbed the marble stairs, and when she reached her mother she took her soft scaly hand and kissed it. A formal gesture, not one of reconciliation. And her mother, in turn, made an assessment – the straggled hair, the torn stockings, the broken arm. Tactful, she determined not to pass comment.

'I needed to come home,' said the woman. There was a long silence. 'Well, meet the children.'

She waved them up the stairs.

'This is Andrew, we call him Andy. Andy, this is your grandmother. Grand-mère. Grandmother.'

He said hello; she smiled.

'And this is Lucy. Lucyloo.'

'Hello Lucyloo,' said Grandmother.

The girl was too shy to reply.

'Will you be staying long?'

A pause. 'Yes, I think so.'

'So, the day of days,' said Grandmother. She tapped one of the balloons with the end of her walking-stick. 'Your brother will be home soon. They are pregnant, you know. In the hospital. We expect them any minute. Everything here is ready, just for the first six months or so – when it's hardest. But, of course, there is plenty of room. Where would you like to sleep, Olivia?'

'Wherever is convenient.'

'Ida will see to it.' She looked to Ida for confirmation. 'Well, come now, are you tired? You must be tired. Such a long trip.' And then she added, '*Was* it a long trip?'

'Very long,' replied the woman. 'Wasn't it, kids?'

The boy shrugged but the girl bobbed her head up and down without stopping.

———◆———

Ida showed them upstairs to their rooms. In the past the children's room had been used for visiting adult guests, for couples who no longer slept together; it was furnished with two large beds, each with a white satin-quilted bedhead. As soon as Ida had left the girl said, 'It smells like old people.' Overcome by an atomic exhaustion – at long last – the woman sank down on an armchair in the corner of the room. The boy bumped on his mattress, gauging its spring. He fiddled with the bedside lamp, twisting the round brass knob beneath a fringed lampshade, but couldn't work out how to turn it on. He stood on the bed and examined the painting that hung above the bedhead – an eighteenth-century portrait of a black-haired, lunar-skinned woman resting a posy of violets in her lap. Violet, the household knew her as Violet. He ran his fingertips over Violet's breasts, feeling the surface of the paint, and used his fingernail to worry off a chip of the craquelure. When he succeeded he proudly held up his finger and showed his mother the chip. 'It's real.'

He jumped down and headed to the long narrow windows that overlooked the great expanse of lawn. He tried everything he could to open the windows but failed.

He twisted himself into the floor-length silk curtains, twisted and twisted, disappeared. It must have been dark in there, so that he could hardly breathe, so that he listened to his heartbeat. After a while the girl – marooned with her doll on her own giant bed – grew frightened.

'Andy!'

He returned to the world.

Glancing at the woman, he walked over to his suitcase and unpacked his mobile telephone and its charger. Contraband. He got down on his knees and, following the cord of the bedside lamp, searched for a powerpoint. As she expected, he found that the prongs of the charger were mismatched and no amount of jamming could fit them into the socket. He sat back on his heels and absorbed the measurements of his confines; he looked deep into each corner as though the junction of two walls, the angle, pointed to a way out. The woman let him be: she hauled herself from the armchair and went next door to her room.

Her room – was never her room. It was another guest room, similarly furnished. She drew the curtains and loosened her hair, freed her arm from its sling. She undressed, dropping all her clothes in a pile on the floor. Crawled onto the bed. Lay belly down, face on the pillow. There was a loop in time; she was already dead. And then she must have sensed the children standing in the doorway for – with great effort, turning her head and opening one eye – she saw reflected in the mirror that, yes, the children had been spying, how long she could not be sure, but they had no doubt seen their mother lying on the bed, the white plain of her back covered in rotten yellowed bruises. 'Andy?' she said and the word sounded strangled, faint. 'You two. Please, go and play outside.'

Not long after Ida was preparing food in the kitchen, an enormous kitchen with a walk-in fireplace, flagstone floor and a long wooden table as its centrepiece. She was working at the table while the twins, the teenage housemaids who had been with her for almost a year, were chopping vegetables on marble-topped benches ranged against the far wall. The children, dutifully in new clothes, stuck their heads around the corner. 'Hello.'

'Hello! Look at you,' said Ida. 'Who is wanting a biscuit?' She only spoke crude English.

The girl held up her doll and stated flatly, 'Her name is Pinky. We're on the run.'

'On the hop,' the boy corrected his sister.

Ida feigned comprehension with an all-purpose smile, gave them each a biscuit. The girl started hopping in a circle.

The boy said, 'We're passing through. Don't worry, we'll be gone soon. Maybe tomorrow. Or the next day.'

The girl, finishing her hopping circle, announced, 'I live in Australia.'

'Australia. Far away. Lots of kangaroos.'

The boy ignored the kangaroo reference and asked, 'Are you a servant?'

In the background the twins suppressed a laugh.

'A housekeeper,' replied Ida. 'And I am here a very long time. I know this place inside outside and I know everything that happens here. Every. Thing. Everything.' She fixed him with a stare she used to scare children. 'The painting. Violet. I know. The curtains. I know.' She tapped her forehead. 'Here, my third eye. Just here.'

She bent down and allowed the children to take turns touching her third eye – just as she had once, many years ago, bent down and allowed their mother the same privilege. In those bygone days the children of the house never doubted Ida's mysterious powers, her affliction; brother and sister had both gone to inordinate lengths to conceal their wrongdoings, even in empty rooms.

'I'll always be watching,' Ida said to the boy, and called to the twins for affirmation. Yes, yes, they nodded in solemn agreement. After the children had gone one of the twins mistakenly slipped an egg yolk onto the bench and, without turning around, Ida clicked her tongue in admonishment.

A little later the children were playing alone by the lake. The boy was skimming stones across the water while the girl dug a hole in the sand, using the plastic hand of her doll as a spade. Weeping willows were married to their reflections. On the far side of the lake, a rippling dark forest, and rising beyond the forest, the mountain – impervious to roads, to tunnels, never to be upended. The woman had changed into a new dress and freshened her make-up, redone her hair. She didn't join the children but instead watched them from a stone bench that overlooked the lake. After a while the girl caught sight of her mother and jumped up, started waving. Ran toward her.

'Mummy!' she grabbed her around the neck. 'Mummy! Can we swim? Can we?'

'It's too cold,' replied the woman. 'The winter's still in the water.'

This scarcely bothered the girl though the boy hung his head and looked like he didn't believe her.

'Oliiiiviiiia! Oliiiiiviiia!'

Ida stood in the distance and waved her white apron over her head. 'Ollliiiiiiviiiiiia!'

They hastened up the path.

'Olivia, come, hurry. Your brother is arriving,' said Ida.

The woman took hold of the girl's hand, Ida took the boy's. They had not gone far before he snatched the girl's doll and broke away, started sprinting.

Inside the house they were obliged to walk through the long parquet hallways at a stately pace: one of the house rules that never must be broken. Grandmother was waiting for them in the entrance hall. They gathered near the door and Ida cupped her hand to her ear. 'Listen.' They listened – they breathed, no-one made a sound. The girl pulled her 'listening face', a kind of grotesque where she clamped shut her eyes and clenched her jaw in a maniacal grin. This lasted about a minute.

'Can you see?' she whispered to Ida.

Yes, she nodded. 'They're coming.'

They heard – a car rasping on the pebbled allée, a car door open and close, footsteps, and – a knock, a knock, a knock. When Grandmother gave the signal, a discreet wave of the hand, Ida opened the door.

'Marcus!' She threw her arms around him. He was tall and had a permanently lowered head so that he always appeared as sheepish. With pale brown hair and blue-grey eyes he was closer in likeness to his late father than to his mother. His father's son. Usually he would have been thought of as handsome but here he was – haggard. Unshaven; grey pouches below his eyes. A cloth baby-bag in a teddy bear print was slung over his shoulder.

'And Sophie!' From the red blotches on her skin it was clear she had been crying. She was in her late thirties and though she was big-boned – solid and wide-hipped – she had somehow made herself very small, almost to the point of disappearing. She was carrying a bundle wrapped in a pale pink blanket close to her chest. On her wrist, the hospital's plastic ID bracelet.

'Olivia?' Marcus asked quietly, but without a note of surprise, as if he could no longer be surprised, had lost this luxury.

'Hello Marcus.' A small gentle smile.

'Hello.' He seemed unsure of what to do then put an arm around Sophie's shoulders, shepherded her through the double doors into the salon. The room was sparely furnished with a few Louis XV pieces, the cabriole legs of the chairs ending in little deer feet. Dozens of antler trophies were collected on the walls. Even with this furniture the room felt empty – in the way an empty room can be made emptier by the addition of a single table. Sophie settled herself on the end of a chaise longue, gingerly; after the birth there must have been stitches or perhaps a bruised coccyx. Grandmother sat opposite her, and Ida stood behind Grandmother, as was her place.

Marcus rested a hand on Sophie's shoulder. 'We . . . I am so sorry to tell you . . .' He looked to the children and hesitated, went on. 'There has been an accident. The cord – as she was born the cord caught around her neck. There was nothing anyone could do. Our beautiful child, our Alice, has died. Did not live.'

After a long pause Grandmother made the sign of the cross. 'Marcus, Sophie,' she said. 'We are so sorry. I . . . I . . . Is . . .?'

'The hospital told us . . . Sophie wanted . . . They said it would be best to bring Alice home.'

'Oh.' Grandmother rearranged her hands in her lap. 'The cord? But in the hospital? How . . .?'

'It just happened,' he said. 'We don't know how. No-one did anything wrong.'

The woman said, 'I am deeply sorry for your loss.' She lowered her head and nodded to Sophie.

'How long will the, the . . .?' Grandmother fumbled.

'A day or two.' He and Sophie exchanged glances. 'We'd like to get to know her before the funeral.'

At the word 'funeral' Sophie baulked and shifted the bundle from one breast to the other.

The top of Ida's knuckles showed white. With a brisk flick of the wrist she caught the woman's attention and indicated that the children should immediately leave the room.

At morning tea-time Ida accompanied the woman to the rose garden; she had readied a tray, with tisane and an almond friand. The woman walked slowly, as if the broken arm had slightly altered her balance and her footfall was no longer automatic, was deliberate. The garden had been a favourite spot of hers as a girl.

So many roses, roses trained to pillars and – when in bloom – cascading from wire umbrellas. Rugosa, Madame Alfred Carrière, Amiga Mia, Parkdirektor Riggers. There was a yellow-tipped rose named after her, the Olivia. Ida set the tray down on one of the wooden seats, the back of which was carved into the shape of fern fronds, and departed.

The woman warmed her hand on the tea-plunger. Then she lifted the object, very carefully, moved it through the air, this glass-and-silver invention, and slowly poured. She poured the tea right to the golden rim of the teacup. Her left-handedness slowed her down, and each gesture, normally habitual, unnoticed, careless, was now new to her, not entirely new, but was seen in a new light, or was seen as if she had – for the first time in her life – lifted from the root of her being, taken a step aside. And there was an element of wonder in her movements, that all along she'd had a left-hander inside. She set down the plunger and brought the teacup to her lips, steady, not spilling a drop. She savoured the tea and then at the same glacial pace settled the cup. She picked up the friand. Heard footsteps; Marcus had found her.

'Mother was right,' said the woman, not looking at her brother but staring into the garden. 'I married a brute.' There was a long pause and then she declared, simply, 'I am murdered.'

Marcus gave a slight nod of the head to indicate he had heard her. She returned the friand to the tray. He sat down beside her and handed her the teacup.

'We tried so hard,' he said, and he too stared ahead, over the roses. 'There was . . . another woman. There is . . . another woman. A foreigner, a musician on scholarship. Very little money. She'll have to go home one day – poor girl. Sophie doesn't know. Maybe she does – she lets me be. I still love her. I just wanted to give her what she has always wanted. For two years she endured nightmares – drugs, hormones, side-effects, more drugs to counter those effects, operation operation operation. The things she did. Everything, everything, on a schedule. Nothing natural about it. No happy accident. And when the baby was conceived we both thought it was – a miracle. I held my breath for the first three months. Every day for three months and every day after that I still feared . . . Only when we got to the hospital did I feel safe.'

The woman had finished her tea but held the cup suspended in mid-air as if this helped her to listen. He turned to her and gently removed the cup. 'Out of my hands.'

He lay down on the bench and rested his head in her lap. For a long time she stroked the hair silvered at his temples. 'Oh,' she murmured. 'Poor boy.'

———

In the entrance hall Grandmother was supervising the twins as they removed the balloons. One of the twins cringed each time she went to stick a balloon, leaning back as if the pop, the noise, could hurt her. After a while she summoned her courage and let fly. The other twin was untying and popping those balloons secured to the staircase. Amused by her sister's antics she let her attention slip and in that moment one balloon escaped to the ceiling. Inhale – she covered her mouth in horror. Grandmother frowned. They watched the balloon bump along the ceiling and come to rest in a corner.

At lunchtime the twins were on their best behaviour. They had set the walnut dining table so that it was resplendent. The finest snow-white linen had been aired and ironed, and they had dusted off a grove of cut-crystal glasses. The silver cutlery was polished and shining. Grandmother reigned at the head of the table, and everyone else was there. Sophie, in a new dress and neatly made up, had brought along the bundle and was cradling it in the nook of her arm. She still wore her hospital ID bracelet as if at any minute something could go horribly wrong. A twin held the silver tureen and Ida ladled out asparagus soup. When all the bowls were full Grandmother said grace. 'Bless-this-food-to-our-use, and-us-to-thy-service, and-make-us-ever-mindful-of-the-needs-of-others. Amen.' Quickly, under her breath. And she alone had her eyes closed, the others not being concerned to feign participation.

They began to eat in silence. Straight-backed, elbows off the table. The boy was spreadeagled over his bowl, slurping the soup into his mouth. Mouthful after mouthful, as if he hadn't eaten in a long while. 'Andrew,' said Grandmother. She lifted her spoon and demonstrated how to use it correctly, how to make a shallow scoop toward the outer edge of the bowl, to bring the spoon to the mouth, not the mouth to the spoon. 'You see.' He tried to copy her, took tiny bird sips, and the girl tried too. But her concentration was broken when she noticed Sophie dipping her little finger into the soup and bringing it to the bundle, trying to feed it. This mesmerised the girl; the others did their best to carry on as though nothing were wrong, the woman spooning her soup with her left hand, like a scientist taking an infinitesimal measure, and Grandmother sighing when at last Sophie wiped her finger on a serviette and reached for her glass of water.

The telephone rang. It was rare for the telephone to ring in the house, and as for an interruption during the lunch hours, it happened once or twice a year. Ida sent a twin to answer the call. The woman was snap-frozen by the persistent ringing, her spoon airborne, and she spilt some soup on the table. Marcus, too, was on edge, and looked ready to stand and answer the call himself. Only the boy's eyes were shining. As soon as the ringing stopped an unsteady peace descended and all resumed eating.

The boy checked his watch and said to his mother, 'At home it's four in the morning.'

The girl said, breezily, by-the-way, 'Andy, I can smell your vulva.'

Ha. 'I don't *have* a vulva.'

The girl, furious, turned to the woman for support in this battle. Just then the twin returned to the room and the moment she took up her position by the commode the telephone rang again. Brrrrrrrring: it had dominion. Off she went. The girl was tugging at her mother's sling, wanting her opinion, but the woman waited and waited and waited for the ringing to stop before she responded.

'He's right,' she said. 'Only girls have vulvas.' At this news the little one was downcast.

And the telephone rang again. One ring. And another. And one more ring. As if it were repeatedly being picked up and immediately put down again.

Marcus tried to strike up a conversation. 'Andy, have you been down to the boathouse?'

'No. There's a boat?' Interested, on the alert.

'Not a boat-boat. But some old canoes. Mother, is that right? Are there still the canoes?'

'I believe so.'

Again, the twin was restored to the room. This time Marcus did make to stand.

'Excuse me,' she said. 'I could not understand the gentleman, my English is poor. I have requested him to not derange the lunch. To call later.'

Very slowly, the woman reached for her wineglass, as if there were a mountain range between her hand and the glass that could only be negotiated with utmost concentration.

Marcus sat down, relaxed. 'Maybe I can take you out on the water?'

The boy nodded. Okay.

'Can I come?' asked the girl.

'We'll see,' said Marcus.

'Mummy, will you come?'

The woman shook her head. 'I don't swim.'

'She means she can't swim,' said the boy, scornful. 'She's afraid of the water.' He paused. 'And escalators.' Another pause. 'And elevators.' He held out two hands and mimed elevator doors closing on his nose, grinned. He looked to his mother and made a loop-the-loop loopy sign by his temple. But she drank her wine and did not chastise him.

Grandmother turned to Marcus. 'Remember Tahiti?' He did not reply. She turned to the boy. 'When your mother was about . . . about Lucy's age, we all went to Tahiti. A special treat. The sand is black in Tahiti. And the men wear straw skirts. That's right. And the minute we saw the sea the child started screaming. Screaming. And screaming. As if the water, the sea, was the most terrifying thing in the world. Those little waves. One after the other. Well,

I walked into the water with her – holding her up high, quite safe, perfectly safe – and she screamed and screamed. I'd never heard a child scream so long before. It was only the sea. Incredible.'

There was a thorough silence. The woman betrayed no reaction other than to keep her eyes trained on the centre of the table.

The telephone rang again. Grandmother snatched up her serviette.

The boy jumped to his feet. 'I'll get it!'

'Sit down.' His mother stood, said, 'May I be excused.'

She did not run along the hallway. She walked as if she had already walked a thousand miles and the hallway were the beginning of a further thousand miles before her. The telephone was crouched on a semicircular bureau in an alcove. A deer head had been mounted on the wall at eye level, giving the impression, at times, that the interlocutor was the deer himself speaking. She picked up the receiver and brought it to her ear. She listened for a few minutes, her features softening, losing form, and then – without speaking – she placed the receiver on the bureau, left it off the hook. She got down on her hands and knees, which was awkward with her cast, and fumbled around trying to unplug the cord. When she had done this she wriggled back out, and then had second thoughts, wriggled back under. She rested her weight on her cast and reached back with her left hand and removed her shoe. With her high heel she pounded the plastic telephone connector, damaging it so that it no longer quite fitted the socket. Finished, she wriggled out again, got to her feet, straightened her skirt and returned the receiver to its cradle.

'Ida.' Grandmother indicated her glass was empty.

The girl was chit-chattering. 'Because I can swim. I can swim. In my carnival I got a blue ribbon, which is first. It's in my bedroom. For fifteen metres. That's across the pool, not down the pool. You go across the pool. I beat Maxie and Beebee and Helen and . . .'

The woman slipped in and found her seat at the table.

Despite inquiring glances from Marcus and the boy no questions were asked. She picked up her fork and placed it in the fingers of her right hand that were peeking out of her cast. She held the fork steady and with her left hand began to patiently cut away a slice of duck.

'Mummy, I'm a good swimmer aren't I?' asked the girl.

The woman nodded.

The girl, now bored, used her knife to smear the potato mash over every inch of her plate. Lay down the knife. She stared at the bundle, was transfixed.

'I want Pinky.'

'After lunch, darling,' her mother replied quickly.

Marcus checked on Sophie. Sophie, who had not said a thing the entire meal, who had not eaten, who had died every time her husband found words – 'boat', 'canoe' – sailing away from her on this 'boat', this 'canoe', so soon, leaving her with their baby. Sophie glared and clambered out of her seat, hurriedly left the room.

'I'm sorry, Mother,' said Marcus. 'It wasn't my idea, Sophie insisted. And, well, if I'd asked what would you have said?'

Grandmother gave this due consideration.

He continued. 'I have a favour to ask you. Olivia'.

———•◦•———

After lunch it was arranged that the woman would be driven to the village; one of the gardeners offered to be the chauffeur. The children and Ida rode with her just as far as the great gateway, the girl squirrelled on Ida's lap so as to save room. Goodbye, goodbye. The boy climbed up the iron filigree. They watched until the car disappeared from view.

'How far can you see?' asked the girl.

'Oh, very far,' said Ida.

'As far as Sydney?'

'Not that far, not across the ocean.'

Oh. They began the long walk back up the driveway.

The ugly countryside was momentarily interrupted by the small ugly village. At the Town Hall the woman sat in a waiting room with an elderly couple for whom waiting seemed to be an end in itself, so that if they weren't waiting in a waiting room they would have been waiting at home in the kitchen or in the bedroom. She noticed earlier visitors had stubbed their cigarettes out on the plastic plant beside her; the leaves were stippled with dark round holes. There were magazines on a small table, personal-investment and travel magazines, a magazine which promised to tell all about the diet of an Olympic swimmer, but she chose to ignore them. After a while a young pregnant woman was shown out of the office. Josette remained at the door. 'Olivia?' These two had played together as children at the local school and in those times Josette had also been invited to the château. She was slightly older than the woman, and though she had been a bureaucrat for many years she had maintained – or had developed – the demeanour of a sincere and kindly nurse.

'Hello Josette.' Softly spoken in French, without trace of an accent.

Josette pulled out a seat for the woman, did not

comment on the broken arm. She sat behind her desk and clasped her hands together, making a temple with her index fingers.

'I'm here to ask permission – the family would like permission to bury another body, at home, next to my father.'

'I heard the sad news. I'm very sorry. Please send my condolences to all concerned. I have already prepared the paperwork. There should be no problem.'

The finger-temple collapsed and she pushed some sheets of paper across the table. 'If you could sign here – and here.'

The woman parsed the paperwork, and when she was halfway down the second page she stopped and asked, 'One body?'

Josette tipped her head and looked to the woman for clarification.

'And Mother has not been well.'

There was a long pause before Josette said, 'Yes, I see, we can change this to . . .' she crossed something out with her pen, 'two bodies.'

The woman signed the bottom of the page with her clumsy left hand and before handing it over studied her signature as if it were a child's attempt at forgery or, worse, a black-lettered joke, a feeble excretion.

'About the baby,' said Josette. 'I believe there would be a good case for negligence. A strong case. In a week or two come back, this should not be forgotten.'

'Thank you Josette, I will mention it to Marcus. And there's the other matter, the children.'

'Ah yes. Yes, yes, yes. Yes, I received your letter last month.' She reached for a manila folder in a staggered wire file of dozens of folders and opened it on her desk. 'Quite a surprise. Andrew? Lucy? Are you sure?'

'Yes.' She quickly opened her handbag and dug around inside, produced two passports.

Josette flicked through the passports and kept them on her side of the table. 'X-rays?'

The woman handed over an envelope. 'I had to fold them, please excuse the creases.'

'The blood and urine?'

Another small package was produced.

'Good,' said Josette. 'Today I will accept these. That's that. They will be residents in no time. Don't worry, I will personally make sure to see this through to the prefecture.'

'Thank you.'

'And school? And what about the school?'

'Les Quatre Vents.'

'The boarding school?'

'Yes. The arrangements are in place.'

Josette wrinkled her nose. 'I hear it is a good school. The headmistress, well, she is . . . But yes, it's a good school. Although for me, the local school is the best. And term begins when? In four weeks. Do they speak any French?'

'A little. I've been practising with them since they were born. They understand a lot, more than they can say. And the school is bilingual. They will learn.'

'They will learn. So, the marvellous capacities of children. Imagine if we could be children again. I would speak five languages. Mandarin. Even Hungarian. Though maybe I wouldn't feel the need to. Impossible to know. Sometimes I wish I'd never stopped somersaulting.

Anyway, please, again – your signature.' She passed more papers across the table and the woman carefully inked her name.

'Thank you, Josette, thank you for everything. You've been very kind to me.'

'It is good to see you, Olivia.'

In the pharmacy she waited for Dr Steenbohm, a tiny elfin man, to finish serving a customer.

'Good afternoon, Dr Steenbohm.'

'Good afternoon. And what a pleasure – but at such a time . . . My condolences to the family. How do you make You Know Who laugh?' She did not answer. 'You make plans. Believe me, I know it. No?' He sighed, continued. 'And your mother? How is she?'

'She is as well as can be expected.'

'These shocks are not good.'

The woman handed him some prescriptions. 'Will you fill these, please?'

He examined the scripts and rubbed his eye, an atavistic gesture of pharmacist's suspicion.

'I got them in Australia,' said the woman. 'When I have a chance I'll come back with a replacement script, something official.' She was very calm, very patient.

'These painkillers – yes. But the digitalis, this is highly restricted.' He flapped the script. 'This is for?'

'For me. To slow the heart. Tachycardia.' She fluttered the fingers of her right hand against her chest.

He hesitated and only when a bell tinkled to signal that he had a new customer did he move to the little storeroom behind him. He returned with two bottles of tablets.

'Be a good girl. Take care.'

'Thank you. Goodbye, Dr Steenbohm. It has been a pleasure.'

As soon as she was outside she shoved the bottles deep into her bag.

It had rained – a sun-shower – and the wet black macadam reflected the sky so that she seemed to be walking on a thin crust over vertiginous depths. A teenager on a scooter was bearing toward her and on instinct she moved to the left side of the pavement but her instinct was wrong and they nearly collided. There was a kebab shop not far from the pharmacy and she crossed in front of it before back-tracking and looking in through the window. A smooth large hunk of processed meat, skewered on a metal pole, was rotating slowly beside a grill, the fat dripping off the meat and collecting in a tray below. Because it was late in the afternoon the shop was empty; a lone attendant in a footballer's tracksuit was reading a newspaper behind the high counter. She went inside and read the chalkboard, perused the bains-marie. On talkback radio a man requested a love song.

'A merguez roll, please.'

'Yes, Madame.'

She took a seat at the only table in the place, squeezed in behind the door. The illuminated drinks refrigerator next to her threw a blue light. He brought her over her roll: two pizzles of red merguez in a pale white bun, some shredded lettuce.

'Thank you.'

She dripped mustard on the bun and picked it up in

one hand, wrapping her fingers around it, trying to hold it together. She savoured each mouthful. She chewed slowly as if the flavour were unknown to her and she wanted to fix it permanently to her palate, leave a lasting impression. From time to time she put down the bun and with a paper napkin she daubed away the halo of grease and mustard around her mouth. When she was finished she took her plastic plate back over to the counter.

'Thank you.'

'You're welcome.'

She found her wallet and paid with a note, not waiting for the change. After she had gone he looked down at the note and raised his eyebrows in surprise at its value.

She went into the bank. The ceiling was decorated with red and green streamers and little cards in the shape of Christmas baubles which read '6.5%'. She joined the long queue for the reception desk. The bank manager, who was sitting with a client in his glass-walled office, looked over and spied the woman. To the confusion of the client this meeting was immediately terminated and the manager hurried away. He approached the woman in the queue, smiling obsequiously and even bowing.

'Good afternoon.'

'Good afternoon.'

'My apologies, I wasn't expecting you quite so soon. The new assistant loves to make mistakes in my diary.'

'No, no, my apologies. There was a change in plans.'

'Well, I'm very pleased to see you. A pleasure.'

'Thank you.'

'Please,' he said, extending his arm – a monogram, cufflinks. 'Won't you come with me. Let's get your affairs in order.' He escorted her into his office.

———

At twilight the car pulled around behind the château. It was that time of day when the last of the light has been absorbed into the sky and darkness has begun to settle on all solid things below, turning the tops of the trees into iron filings drawn starward. Ida was in the kitchen while the twins were in the laundry. Sophie was on the lawn, lying on a picnic blanket with her bundle; she had been out there most of the afternoon. When the woman left the car she caught sight of Sophie and watched as she tentatively lifted the bundle over her head and moved it through the air. With her arms still outstretched Sophie craned her neck and faced the woman, although at a distance and in the darkening neither could make out the other's expression. They stayed like this – one the beginning and one the end of a connection made manifest – until, as if she had only just been caught out staring, the woman turned on her heel and snapped the connection, walked away.

Marcus came into the kitchen holding a pink satin ballgown that had belonged to his mother and smelt of musky perfume and mothballs. Ida, confused, smoothing the flat of her apron, asked what he was doing. Before he could answer the woman entered and said, 'I remember that dress. I wanted to wear it to my sixteenth birthday party but when I tried it on I couldn't do up the buttons. Even though I was one of the skinniest girls in class. I couldn't believe Mother had ever been able to fit it.'

Marcus said, 'I remember. And you wore a yellow dress instead. It made you look beautiful.'

'Thank you.' She continued, 'I've spoken with the Town Hall. Everything is in order. Please let me know how else I can be of help.'

'Thank you, Olivia.'

'The children?'

'Upstairs. Sleeping.'

When she had left, Marcus lay the dress on the kitchen table. He went to the drawers and found a pair of scissors, laid these side by side with the dress.

'Ida, there is something I need you to do. I'll help you. The baby – the doctors said . . .' His voice trailed off and then he blurted out, 'She has to sleep in the freezer.'

'The freezer?' Incredulous.

'The doctors said —'

'No.' Ida shook her head. 'No. I refuse.'

'To keep —'

'No. I refuse.'

'Because the —'

'No.'

'Doctor's orders.'

'No.'

'Ida, we have no choice.'

'No.'

He sighed and walked over to the upright silver freezer. He began removing the frozen food, stacking it neatly on one of the benches. She watched him. Did not help. When he had emptied the freezer of its contents he gathered up the dress and the scissors.

'And we have to make it – comfortable.'

He returned to the freezer and held out the dress, measured it against the door. When his back was turned Ida took a plate and dashed it to the floor.

———

The children's room was a pigsty: suitcases disembowelled, bedspreads kicked to the floor, Violet hung askew. The woman stood in the doorway and watched the children sleeping; they'd tossed off most of their clothes. The girl was splayed horizontally across her mattress, the boy had his feet pointed to the bedhead. Through the window: evening star. The girl rolled over in her sleep. Quietly shutting the door behind her and picking her way through the room, the woman carefully lay down beside the girl, making sure not to touch her. She curled onto her side and used her left upper arm as a pillow, closed her eyes. Opened them again. Let the lids fall. A moment later the boy did a sudden flip-flop, realigning himself so that he no longer faced in her direction.

They slept and their breathing was slow and steady. When the girl babbled something incoherent, sleeptalking, they slept through it. And in sleep they looked just the same as they had looked the last time they'd slept, in another country, under another roof, as if the sleeping state were one to be returned to – effortlessly transcending timelines and territories – rather than encountered. Suddenly the woman jolted awake – perhaps she'd had a dream in which she was falling. The room was dark. She switched on the bedside lamp and checked her wristwatch: nearly three hours had passed. She sat on the edge of the bed and vigorously rubbed one eye as though she hoped to drag it down to her chin. She went over to the boy and gripped his shoulder, shook him awake. He was wild-eyed, startled, but even before his mother could say anything he had already taken stock, as if it were only the being ripped out of deep sleep that had shocked him and not any prospect that lay ahead – in this regard he was a veteran.

'It's okay,' said the woman. 'Time to get up. We can't sleep, it's bad for jetlag. Up you get. Get dressed.'

He got to his feet, uncomplaining.

The woman bent over the girl and stroked her hair. Gently began tapping on her cheek. 'Lucy . . . Lucyloo.'

'I'm asleep,' said the girl, eyes closed. 'Sleeeeeepy.'

The woman kept tapping at her cheek, her eyelids. 'If you sleep now you won't sleep all night. And we need dinner. I'm tired too – but we have to stay up a bit before we can sleep. Okay? Like I told you.'

The girl squeezed her eyes closed and blindly batted away her mother's hand.

'Where's Pinky?' said the woman. 'Here she is. Hello

Pinky. See, Pinky's awake.'

The girl sat up and grabbed Pinky. The woman leant down and found a dress on the floor for the girl. 'Here you go darling, you'll look lovely.'

The children dressed, laced their shoes. The woman took hold of the doll and held it to her ear. 'What's that? One more dream. Alright Pinky.' She turned to the girl. 'Let's tuck Pinky in.'

They lay the doll on the pillow, pulled up the sheets.

'Sweet dreams,' said the woman. The girl gave her doll a kiss on the plastic dome of its forehead. 'Sweet dreams.'

———

In the hallway they stopped before an arrangement of flowers – pink roses, lilies, peonies – that sat on a marble table in the shape of a half-moon. The vase was made of cut crystal and was etched all around with a line an inch or so from the lip: the water-line. The girl tugged at her mother's skirt. The woman reached out her hand and pressed her thumbnail into a rose petal; it didn't leave a mark. She slipped a finger below the water-line and felt that the vase was empty.

The woman led the children to the kitchen. One of the twins was doing the last of the washing up; everything else had been cleared away. A bucket was stationed below the pipes of the sink. 'Oh! Hello!' she said in surprise. 'We thought you were . . .' She fished for the English word but to no avail, made a pillow with her wet hands and brought it to her cheek.

'Sleeping,' said the woman.

'Yes. Everyone is eaten. Oh – please. Please sit down. One moment.'

She made her way to the fridge, the tall stainless steel fridge that stood as companion to the freezer, and hesitated before opening the door as if inside there lurked a razored jaw, a monster. She gathered the food very quickly. Shut tight the door. A deep breath escaped her. She returned to the sink and began to unwrap the roasted chicken from its topcoat of foil. The woman and the children slid onto the low bench at the table.

The girl struck a geyser of enthusiasm: 'I scream! You scream! We all scream for ice-cream!'

'Why not?' said the woman, rising. 'You've been such a good girl today.'

The twin looked at her in dismay. 'Madame!'

But it was too late. The woman crossed the room and opened the freezer door, just a fraction. Spied the pink satin. Slammed it shut. The boy, too, had seen something – out of the corner of his eye, something colourful – he couldn't be sure exactly what; maybe he saw something maybe he didn't, maybe something accounted for his mother's reaction or maybe it didn't.

'Uh-oh,' said the woman. 'No ice-cream. But what's this . . .?' She opened the fridge and, using her shoulder as a wedge, rummaged around inside. 'What's in here . . .? Hey presto . . . chocolate cake.' She held the cake aloft. 'For after dinner.'

'Yabbayabba yum-yum!'

The boy said nothing.

Much relieved, the twin hurriedly brought over plates of cold roasted chicken, buttery leeks.

'Here for you,' she said to the children. 'Bon appétit.'

'Bon appétit,' they replied in automatic sing-song and then, surprised at themselves, offered shy smiles.

'Thank you,' said the woman. 'It's late, please don't let us keep you. But before you go – do you think Mother is awake?'

'Oh yes, certainly. She never . . .' miming sleep with her hand-pillow. 'At the most she,' repeating the gesture, 'for two or three hours. Like Napoleon. Oh yes, at this hour she will be living.'

'Thank you. You've been a great help. Good night.'

'Good night.'

The woman looked down to her plate. They listened to the drips collecting in the bucket. The children waited for her to start to eat. 'Well,' she said. 'Go on.'

———

Up the stairs, along the hallway, turning right, turning right again, turning left until they reached a door. The woman buzzed the intercom, holding the button down a long time. They waited. She pressed again.

'Yes?' Grandmother's voice sounded scratchy and far-away, as though she were an astronaut or mountain guerrilla.

The woman leaned forward and spoke directly into the intercom. 'Mother, it's me. With the children. To say good night.'

'Come in.' There was a buzz and a click.

They walked through a suite of three enormous rooms, low-lit, one room opening out onto the other via a pair of double doors. Each room was elegantly, if minimally, furnished. A pair of Qing dynasty glazed porcelain vases, kingfisher-blue. A silken Persian carpet. A giant plasma screen flat to one wall. And there were secret doors in the walls of the rooms, secret doors leading to secret servant passages, now spidered and empty.

'Errh.' The boy bent down to inspect what he had accidentally trodden on: a raw chicken wing. He used his fingers as pincers and held it up to show his mother. With his top teeth he made a rabbitty overbite and at the same time scrunched up his nose – 'Disgusting.' Half-eaten raw chicken wings were littered all over the floor. A Burmese cat on top of a footstool observed the intruders.

Grandmother was in the third room. She was propped up in her great bed which had a curved footboard inlaid with lozenges of tulip and rosewood in the shape of prancing deer. She'd removed her make-up and smothered her eyebrows in white cold-cream. Her white cotton nightdress had a high frilled collar which tied under the chin. At the end of the bed there was a small TV nestled in a walnut cabinet – switched on but with the volume turned down low.

'Come here Lucyloo,' said Grandmother, patting a spot on the bed. 'Andrew, come over here.' She picked up a cat, another Burmese who had been lying by her side, and brandished it high for their inspection. 'This is Hello.' She turned the cat toward her, cooed 'Hellooo. You're such a good cat. A lovely good cat. Hellloooo. Aren't you.' She rubbed the cat in her face; the woman watched with equanimity. 'Oh yes you are. Hellooooo.'

The boy said, 'Grandmother, can I stroke your pussy?' Victory. His mother shot him a dark look.

'Of course!' said Grandmother. 'Here we go. Lovely and soft.' The children took turns stroking the cat between the ears.

'Helllooo! Helllooo!' said the girl, staring intently into its eyes like a hypnotist. 'Helloooo!' She grinned, delighted by the cat, and took her mother's left hand, ferrying it over to the animal, a limp offering. After a moment the woman gently withdrew the hand.

'Good night Mother.'

'Good night,' said the children. They both gave Grandmother a peck on the cheek.

In their wake the TV came alive.

Behind a door: Sophie was in her room, sitting on the very edge of her bed. Not moving, as though there were nothing behind her and if she lay back she would only tumble through depthless space, over and over. She was half dressed, in her skirt and stockings, her high heels. And on top, wearing a sturdy white bra, the kind designed for breastfeeding. Wet stains pooled around her nipples. Marcus, in pyjamas, came to sit close beside her. He, too, sat very still, an audience member watching an invisible movie projected on the wall. After a while he reached across and tenderly brushed a loose strand of hair away from her face, tucked it behind her ear. She turned to him and, without saying anything but imploring, imploring this man her husband, she slowly placed his hand on her wet nipple. Then she reached her other hand around behind his neck and gently guided his head down to her warm breast. Fumbling, he unpopped the press studs on the flap of the bra. He took her nipple into his mouth and suckled. The house was quiet. The night worked night magic. Far away an owl called.

In the morning the boy's bed was empty. The girl was fast alseep, oblivious to the daylight. He wasn't in his mother's room, nor in the kitchen. Not in any room downstairs. He wasn't behind the curtains. Nor in any of the cupboards. In the garden the dew sparkled on the spiderwebs, countless fine spiderwebs in the grass and caught between the rosebushes, all to disappear by noon. He had disappeared.

But not through the door in the wall, now boarded up from the inside. The birds were making busy. He was by the lake, in the boathouse, tinkering around. The air was cool and dank; there were mouldy canvases crumpled over unknown objects on the stone floor, nests of old rope and cord. Two canoes lay face-down on a slatted wooden platform, boy's-chest-high. Both were made from bottle-green fibreglass although one had seen more use, was patched and peeled. With fingers spread wide the boy raked a pattern through the dust on the smooth hull of the unblemished canoe. He lifted one end and tried to look up inside it: a mouse ran out and he let the canoe fall. He tried again, jacking the end up as high as he could, and this time the canoe slid backwards – he struggled to hold it, gripped it by the rim, he struggled, he held it, he held it high, he tried, he struggled to hold it – it clattered to the ground. On reflex, he quickly looked over his shoulder to see if anyone was watching.

He knelt by the fallen hull and began to inspect it for damage. There was a voice outside, a man's voice, indistinct.

He ran and hid behind the door, peered out through the crack, spied. Marcus was pacing to and fro on the thin fringe of grey sand that encircled the lake. Each time he came closer to the boathouse the boy could make out a word or two – 'my love', 'my darling', 'soon'. Walking away, Marcus nodded his head and then he held the phone far from his ear, let the lake listen. That morning the surface of the water was smooth, not uniformly smooth but made up of large patches of smoothness. After a minute or so he began to talk and pace once more. He stopped – his back to the boy – and expertly unzipped his cream linen trousers, hunched his shoulders and slightly bent his knees. The tip of his elbow jigged up and down, up and down, until he suddenly straightened, lifted his heels. He talked a little longer then zipped up his trousers. Pocketed the phone. He shook out his arms and legs as if he were coming indoors after a sun-shower. Then he turned to face the boathouse – square on – so that it seemed he was staring straight at the boy. To the boy's consternation, Marcus decided to pay a visit.

'Oh – good morning.' Marcus was surprised to find the boy deep in concentration, tying knots in a rope.

'Hi,' said the boy, feigning disruption. There was a long pause in which neither wanted to risk giving themselves away and then the boy said quietly, 'I'm sorry about the baby.'

'Thank you.' His smile was almost apologetic. Something like sorrow passed between them and in that moment they were mountain and lake, ancient. 'Well,' said Marcus, finally summoning a jolly note. 'What have you got there?'

The boy showed him the little reef-knot.

'Not bad. And what about this pair of beauties?' said Marcus, nodding to the canoes. 'What do you say – shall we go out later on the water?'

'Okay.'

'Okay, okay, it's a deal then,' he said, rolling back his sleeves. 'Come on, let's carry this one out, you and me.' He squatted down on his heels and rubbed his palms together. 'You ready?'

Together they carried the fallen canoe lakeside, laid

it to rest. A scurf on the sand showed that the lake had its own currents, was never entirely still.

'Phase one,' said Marcus. 'Mission accomplished.' He smiled.

'Is that your phone?' said the boy, pointing to the pocket.

'Yes, it's a phone. No, it's a car. A phone.'

'Can I please borrow it?'

Marcus thought a while before answering. 'To call Australia?' He paused. 'It doesn't work. No international service. My wife banned me because of the high bills. Too bad for us, hey.' He softly cuffed the boy on the jaw. 'Come on, let's go. Breakfast.'

It was unwelcome news, a rumour received by a soldier.

———•———

In the breakfast salon a vine had been allowed to creep up the wall and along the cornice. Plants spilled from ceramic pots on wooden tripods, from hanging cane baskets. A round table covered in a blue-and-white embroidered cloth had been set with breakfast things: a silver pot of coffee, the pot standing on skinny bird legs, clawed bird feet; croissants; jams; a pat of butter; a bowl of hard-boiled eggs. Some toast. Apples and oranges. Some milk, some sugar, the morning's plenitude. Laid everywhere: windowfuls of light. The girl sat at the table, and Pinky was there too, atop a pile of cushions in her own chair. The woman was slowly flipping the pages of a newspaper, just looking at each page as if it were a shopping catalogue or junk mail. Then she closed her eyes and ran her left hand over the type, as though seeking a hidden form of braille. At the sound of footsteps she stopped this experiment. The boys came in.

'Morning all,' said Marcus.

'Good morning,' chimed the woman and the girl in unison.

Marcus and the boy took up their seats and helped themselves to provisions. The woman shunted the newspaper across the table and Marcus briefly scanned the front page which was dominated by a gory photograph, the aftermath of a market explosion. He put it aside.

The girl held up her Bunnykins mug and said to her mother, 'This milk tastes like your arse.'

The woman blinked once or twice and replied, 'You don't know what my arse tastes like.'

'Yes, I do,' said the girl. 'I've smelt it.'

The woman sighed.

'You're disgusting,' said the boy. He took aim and pegged some apple across the table.

'Am not.'

'Are so.'

'Am not.'

'Are so.'

Marcus brought an end to this tiff by asking a general question. 'Has anyone seen Sophie?'

'Not yet,' said the woman.

'Well,' the girl spoke in the tone of a seasoned gossip, 'Ida says . . . Ida says the dead baby is having a bath.' So there. She smirked triumphantly at the boy.

Marcus stood up and said in a low voice, 'May I be excused.'

The woman watched as the girl began to paint her lips with jam. When she raised her dirty hands like lion paws and made a roaring face the woman did not react. The girl didn't seem to care and returned to making a mess with her food. Suddenly she looked up and made the roaring face again, trying to catch her mother off-guard. It made no impression. The girl just shrugged and happily busied herself with her doll.

—————

Later that morning they were all assembled in the summer pavilion, a small stone pavilion supported by nine Corinthian pillars and set on a low rise which gave upon the lotus pond. They were sitting quietly in a circle, on cane chairs that the twins had earlier lugged over from the house. Grandmother was there, in her wheelchair, with Ida standing sentinel behind her. One chair was empty – they were waiting for Sophie. A bird, a swallow, flew through and settled under an eave. The girl started banging her ankles against her chair; the boy rubbed his eyebrows up and over his browbone. Marcus kept checking his watch. A paroxysm: he dug into his pocket as if an insect had bitten him. He removed his mobile phone and made sure to switch it off. Grandmother toyed with the pearls at her throat, then with the golden buttons of her navy jacket; Ida laid a soothing hand on her shoulder. A cool breeze rose and fell and the swallow slid away. The woman watched a beetle cross the floor with brute persistence. Marcus gripped both curved armrests of his chair and made as if to stand – but he thought better of it and sat back down. At last the girl, who had a view in the direction of the house, whispered, 'She's coming.' They all turned to watch as Sophie slowly made her way across the lawn. She was wearing a pale pink dress, silk that fell soft against the skin, and had pinned a flower behind her ear. Lopsided, she carried a white wickerwork bassinet in her hand. She had not removed the hospital ID bracelet.

'Sorry we're late. Thank you for waiting,' said Sophie, bright with bravado. She settled beside her husband and lowered the bassinet to the ground. Sat there. So. Marcus reached over and lightly touched her thigh, lifted out the bundle.

'Yes, thank you for being with us at this special time,' he said. He brought the bundle under his nose, inhaled deeply. 'This is our girl. Alice. She is loved. We will never forget her.'

His eyes glistened and he passed the bundle, the offering, to Grandmother. She clasped it to her chest, rocked back and forth. 'Dear Alice, dear sweet girl, granddaughter. My angel. Angel girl.'

The boy was sitting alongside Grandmother and as she made to pass him the bundle he turned to the woman for reprieve. Her eyes darkened, inclement. He held the bundle awkwardly, as if it were heavy or sharp, and said – looking to the ground – 'Dear Alice. Hello. I'm sorry I didn't get to know you and —'

The girl cried out, 'Pass the parcel! Pass the parcel! Pass —'

The woman gave her a hard slap on the face. There was quiet.

The boy passed the bundle to his mother. Her cast made it difficult and they nearly fumbled the exchange.

'Hello Alice,' said the woman, peeking under the

blanket. 'Black-haired,' she thumbed the eyelids open and closed, 'very beautiful blue-eyed girl.' She looked up to the group and waited for assistance. Marcus came over to relieve her and he knelt before the girl, next in their circle. 'This is Alice. Alice, this is Lucy.'

One look, the horror glimpse, and – unbidden – the girl's face contorted into a fearful cry. She plunged herself into her mother's lap, squeezed her tight. And the boy held his breath and eventually the woman placed a hand between the girl's shoulderblades, let it rest.

Marcus stood up and gently returned the bundle to Sophie, saying, 'Our child.' She took it back, she took the child from him, from them, and she wiped her cheeks and found them wet and that she had been crying.

———

'Never. Never in my day. Never. Holy Mother. Never.'

Ida was at the kitchen bench, muttering as she chopped the leafy greens, chopped with a fury. She shook her head and like some sort of motor this made her chop even faster. 'Never in my day. Never.' The twins were

working alongside her, trying to be invisible. Ida paused
and then slammed down her knife. She went to the back
door and opened it, stealing it away from a delivery-
man who was clutching a huge arrangement of flowers.
He withdrew his knocking fist in surprise. The flowers,
mostly bright orange and purple birds-of-paradise, were
garish and Ida accepted them without comment. One of
the twins said, 'How pretty,' and Ida silenced her with a
glare. She carried the flowers through the house to the
entrance hall and set them on the white marble-topped
side-table. She stood back to study the placement and
saw that the table had become a tomb. No matter which
angle she turned the arrangement, or where on the
table she placed it, the flowers were funereal and ugly.
Muttering, she gathered them up and headed, without
pause, to Sophie's room. No-one was there. She depos-
ited the flowers on a chest of drawers. Outside she spied
Marcus and Sophie on a chequered picnic blanket, reclin-
ing on the lawn. She wiped her hands on her apron,
walked away.

On the lawn: Marcus had a sheet of paper and as he nuzzled the phone to his ear he ticked a series of names off a list. Sophie was lying beside him, the bundle resting in the soft nook of her chest. Marcus made polite listening sounds – mmm, yes, thank you. Later he said, 'Very good, we'll see you tomorrow, the service begins at eleven. Yes, thank you. Most appreciated. Goodbye.'

He switched off the phone and secured it in his breast pocket. To Sophie he said, 'That's done.' They studied each other as though the next thing to say or do might be hinted, revealed. He stood up. This seemed to displease her and she reached out to grab onto the cuff of his trousers, would not let go. At last he relented and sat back down. Sophie held up the bundle and offered, 'See, she has your chin.'

'She does,' he agreed.

With a nod Sophie claimed this as a small victory.

<hr>

After lunch Grandmother asked the woman to take her for a stroll. They went in the wheelchair to the Japanese garden, an enclave of reddish maples and azaleas all shades of pink, of knotweed and crêpe myrtle and magnolia, a colourful relief, the flower of the greater gardens. The criss-crossed rapiers of the cherry blossoms had not yet readied to bud. Grandmother remarked on a stand of bamboo, due to be thinned. They crossed an ornamental wooden bridge, arched over an ornamental pond, the woman pushing the chair so that there was no eye contact between them. On the far side of the bridge a stick caught in the wheel of the chair and held fast, jammed. The woman jolted the chair in an effort to dislodge the stick. She shook the chair, she shoved and jerked it to and fro – untold left-hand strength. Grandmother gripped the sides of the chair as if she were on a rollercoaster. Again the woman jerked the chair. She jerked it and shoved it and tipped it back so that the front wheels looked to be springing into the sky. After a while Grandmother, who had borne this without complaint, flailed one arm upward in order to rein in her daughter. 'Just a minute,' she said, breathless. The woman stopped immediately. Grandmother slowly levered herself out of the chair and stepped aside. The woman crouched down and examined the wheel. She tugged at the stick, mangled in the spokes, tugged and tugged until she succeeded in pulling it free. Grandmother sat back down and they resumed their stroll.

The woman, staring ahead, said, 'Mother, there is something I must say, that I need to ask you. I don't expect, I can't expect your forgiveness, I don't need your forgiveness – it means nothing to me – but I ask that even if I am not remembered in your will that the children are, your grandchildren. Promise me you will look after them.'

Grandmother, also staring ahead, replied, 'They are already remembered. Your brother told me. I have always known.'

This came as news to the woman. Her left hand held the chair steady and they spoke no more.

In the late afternoon the children were playing in the boathouse. The boy was stashing provisions where he could, secreting away little clingwrapped parcels of food, slipping two plastic bottles of water beneath a crush of canvas. The girl, meanwhile, was plaiting and replaiting her doll's hair.

'Ummaaah . . ..' said the girl, drawing out the word with tattle-tale inflection. 'Ida can see.'

The boy carried on. 'Sometimes you're dumb,' he noted.

'Am not,' she said, though quietly, a disinterested defence.

They entertained themselves; they overlooked the hours. She plucked off the doll's head and pushed it down into the plastic funnel of neck so that the doll faced backwards. In a similar fashion she began to reverse the limbs. She had succeeded in disarticulating the right leg when the boy came over and punched her on the arm. 'Come on,' he said. 'Come on.'

They went outside – nightfalling – he led her by the hand. In the distance the mountainside was peppered with points of light. They listened to the lap and lull of the lake. The upturned canoe lay just as he had left it; he flipped it over. He hopped inside and took up a position, ramrod straight like a ship's captain, and then gestured impatiently for the girl to step aboard. 'Go on, get in.' She did this graciously and they sat there for a long time, looking across the darkening water, this vast uncharted ocean, this high sea, this Loch Ness, until the boy, in the sudden way children end their games – without warning – jumped up and over the side. He helped his sister disembark and together they retreated through the garden.

———————

The next morning the house was abuzz in preparation for the funeral.

Upstairs in the children's room the woman was doing her best to fix a thin slip of black satin ribbon in the girl's hair. The girl, clad in her pyjamas, waited patiently, even happily, as the woman tried to fashion a bow.

'Two rabbit ears,' instructed the girl. 'Wrapped on top of each other.' Each determined attempt was a failure but the woman persisted with no show of exasperation – if anything she seemed fascinated by the ingenuity of the knot, by the hair so soft, by this act of decoration. The boy watched his mother's left-handed endeavours and only when she had tried something like ten times did he step forward and say quietly, 'I'll do it.' He tied the bow deftly. The girl spun around and grinned.

'Very pretty,' said the woman in approval. 'Very pretty mississippi.'

The girl blushed and scuffed her toes against the floor in shy delight.

'I have a surprise,' said the woman. 'Come with me.'

The boy stiffened.

From her suitcase she pulled a black velvet dress with a white peter-pan collar. And for the boy – a black velvet suit and a blue-and-white chequered shirt. Cuffs and all. She helped the girl into the dress. But the boy was displeased: the sleeves of his jacket fell well short of his wrist, ridiculous.

The woman sat on the bed and handed a black silk scarf to the boy. He folded it in half, into a triangle. She held out her cast and he slipped it into the sling. She lowered her head so that he could secure the two silken ends. There was a kiss-curl at the snowy nape of her neck and with great care he stuck the tip of his little finger inside it. His mother was beautiful. 'Come on,' she said. He hurriedly fastened the sling and shuffled a few steps back. She rose to her full height and straightened her black fitted dress. 'Are we ready,' she said. 'Let's go then.'

The children refused to leave.

'How fast can you run?' said the woman, adopting a martial tone and pointing her finger at the boy.

'As fast as a leopard.' Glum.

'And how fast *are* you going to run?'

'As fast as a leopard.'

'So – do it then.'

Downstairs, the drawing room that had once played host to soldiers at the end of the war was spruce and clean. The furniture, now liberated from dirty white drop-cloths, had been aired and shined and polished. There was a collection of ancient instruments hung on one wall and high above the ceiling was decorated with faded seascapes of places unknown. At the end of the room a long table had been laid with a row of gleaming silver domes. Ida moved down the buffet, lifting each dome, inhaling, carrying out a final inspection of the labours of the dawn. The twins walked two paces behind her, bunching their hands in their aprons. In skipped the girl – 'Good morning, good morning' – over to Ida, grabbing her by the waist and then pulling away, holding out the hem of her black velvet dress like a sail. Ida and the twins instantly made a great fuss over the girl and allowed her – only if she promised not to touch – to join in the inspection. Ta-da! Under the dome: a gelatinous pink mousse in the shape of a salmon. The boy sought refuge near the tall windows. The first of the chauffeured cars were drawing toward the château, as if the machines themselves knew the slow pace of mourning.

Marcus, in a sombre fine-wool suit, a tie, and clean-shaven, stood by the doorway, ready to greet the arrivals.

They emerged from their cars, ancient men and women; the women were all in hats and some wore veils of black lace, black lace or rotten leaves. These were the blood relatives, the revolution refuseniks, death's attendants. They proceeded one by one up the stairs and when they crossed the threshold each nodded or blinked to Marcus by way of condolence. Marcus, in turn, nodded and said, 'Thank you,' said, 'Please, this way,' said, 'Good morning.' An elderly man in a three-piece suit stopped to pat Marcus on the shoulder. With his ancient gummy mouth he tried to find an ancient word but the struggle was too much for him and he gaped and gaped until his wife tugged at his coat and led him away. Another man bowed deeply. A woman, shrunken to the size of a small child, crushed Marcus's hand. The guests drained through the long corridors and out of the house. For the occasion a path had been marked out with white-painted stones, leading across the lawn and turning up a small hill.

The family plot lay beneath an enormous white oak, a tree that in days of old would have held up the sky. The plot consisted of one headstone and, alongside, a small open grave that smelt of fresh-turned earth. An empty open-lidded walnut casket – tiny, trimmed in satin – rested at the foot of the grave. The woman and the children were waiting nearby, amid the assembled guests. A few of the guests snuck glances at the woman, and then to one another, but the woman did not seem to notice. The boy kept his head down so as to ward off any winks or other familiarities from the old folk. Two gardeners stood at a discreet distance, shovels in hand. At last Grandmother appeared at the bottom of the hill, one of the twins pushing her in the wheelchair. Behind Grandmother came the family priest, broad-shouldered though stooped, alert, his vigour tempered by an ebony walking-cane. Marcus and Sophie followed the priest. In her arms, Sophie nursed the bundle.

They huddled around the open grave. The priest stepped forward and raised his cane.

'Friends,' he said. 'Within the healing embrace of God's love we have gathered here to remember Alice and to entrust her into God's eternal care . . .' He paused. Sophie frowned and sucked in her cheeks.

He continued. 'Knowing that God's good purpose for His people cannot be defeated by sin and death. We are all children of God, and in the faith that God has given to us we turn to God now, asking for His comfort and His grace to be upon us – and to dwell in a special way upon Alice and upon those who were —'

He was interrupted by a loud groan. Sophie turned from the grave and with the bundle still in her arms she bolted in the direction of the house; her gait was pained and awkward. When she reached the bottom of the hill Marcus ran after her. A whisper passed from guest to guest and Grandmother pressed her hand to her heart; she looked to be on the verge of fainting. The boy was delighted and grinned at his sister.

'Please bear with us at this difficult time,' announced the woman.

A breeze bent blades of grass in and out of shadow. Some leaves of the great oak let loose. In time the guests began to shift their weight from foot to foot, to cough and scratch and splutter. Like a flock of birds, they began their departure as if under the one directive.

'Goodbye,' said the woman, holding the fort at the top of the stairs. 'Goodbye, thank you for coming.'

A guest glared at the woman as if she were personally responsible for the scandal. Most hobbled away shaking their heads in commiseration. 'Thank you,' recited the woman. 'Goodbye, thank you for coming.'

One by one the cars defected. The priest was the last through the door. He stood face to face with the woman and tried to pin her with a look of deep sympathy.

'Thank you,' she said flatly. 'Thank you for coming.'

He bowed his head. By the time he was halfway down the stairs she had gone.

———————

In the drawing room the splendid buffet was untouched. The woman was sitting on a small sofa, drinking white wine. An uncorked bottle of Montrachet rested between her knees. She looked up as Marcus entered the room.

'I love to be drunk,' she announced. 'I'm good at it.'

And as if to prove that this was true she bent down and set her cut-crystal goblet on the floor. With her left hand she raised the bottle and began to fill the goblet; she even drew the bottle up and down, stretching the wine. She filled it to the very lip without spilling a drop. Straightening up, she brought the goblet to her mouth and smiled ruefully as though she were a magician who knew her audience could only be pleased by her lesser tricks.

'Where's Sophie?' she asked.

'Sleeping,' said Marcus. 'With pills. And Alice.'

Oh.

'Please – please stay,' said the woman, ultra-lucid. 'I'm drunk. I see everything. I'm on the cusp of the present and the future – the cusp of a great thing, the cusp is the great thing. The world is unfolding before me. Through me. I feel as if – I can see through things. I'm unreasonably happy. But the terrible thing – the terrible terrible thing – is that I am full of love. I'm full of an all-encompassing love for every single thing. I beg you, stay with me, have a drink, please – because I am so full of love and tenderness and forgiveness that I want . . . all I want to do in the world is pick up the phone and call . . . call him, my Murderer. So please, have a drink with your sister.'

Marcus found himself a goblet. He plucked one of the ancient wooden instruments off the wall, something like a small bulbous banjo, and tucked it under his arm. Equipped, he grabbed hold of a dining chair and set it down opposite the woman. They made a silent toast. Then he slid off the chair onto his knees and, still on his knees, shuffled over toward his sister. She bent down and he reached up: he gave her a kiss on the forehead. In his ear she whispered, 'The child's death – it was not your doing.' They were motionless for some time, felt the warmth of the other's breathing. Eventually he swivelled on his knees and returned to his place. He set the instrument on his lap and with his head low, a natural fit, he examined the strings, quickly lifting his eyes to signal a performance for her benefit. It was a tune she immediately recognised from their childhood. He played faster and faster – grinning, nimble, scurrying to keep up with the runaway jig. Listening, she grew radiant.

—•—

The girl had wandered into the garden; she was pushing her pram down a pathway lined with stone obelisks that were covered in a fine furry moss and she had the contented air of someone walking without need of destination. Because there was no-one else around to dwarf her – and because the grandeur of the garden had a miniaturising effect on all who passed through it – the girl appeared to be full-grown. She sallied forth. The poplar trees threw thin afternoon shadows. Out of the corner of her eye she spied something on the lawn. She parked her pram at a safe distance and went to duly investigate. It was a rabbit. Dead for some days. There was a wound on the animal's back and this wound was infested with maggots. She bent over the animal as though to shield it from prying eyes and then examined the waxy maggots at close range. She marvelled at how they curled whenever she would touch them. After a while she tired of the maggot game and abandoned the rabbit. She continued her long walk along the path until it occurred to her to stop, to unbuckle her doll. She held Pinky at arm's length and studied her closely. All of a sudden she opened her hands and let Pinky drop. Keeping her arms outstretched she stared down to the doll on the ground.

———◆———

On her return to the house the girl ran into her brother as though attracted by a sibling valency. He enticed her into the drawing room where the woman lay unstrung on the sofa. Her dress had ridden up toward her hips, revealing a pattern of yellowed bruises on her thighs. Marcus was slumped nearby in his chair, lightly snoring. By his feet were two empty bottles of wine. The children tried to rouse their mother. The girl pulled at her hair and then began to batter her shoulders like a Swedish masseuse. The boy squatted down so that he was level with the woman; he observed her as she scrunched up her eyes and resisted the onslaught. Finally the girl gave up. As they were leaving the room the boy caught sight of the mobile phone in the breast pocket of Marcus's jacket. To the girl's amazement he inched it out, he pinched it. The rise and fall of snoring was constant. She was about to speak but the boy glared and made the gesture of zipping his lips, back and forth, back and forth; he jabbed his thumb over his shoulder.

Upstairs they hid beneath a piano covered in a white drop-cloth; the music room had been closed many years ago. Suddenly the phone began to vibrate. Startled, the boy put it on the parquet floor and they watched it wriggle like a squib. The vibrations stopped for a few moments and then it began to rattle again. This time the boy picked up the phone and held it to his ear. He listened for a while and looked to his sister, making a sick-face by pretending to stick his finger down his throat. He pressed a button and ended the call.

'Who was it? Who was it?' demanded the girl.

He shrugged. 'A ka-ray-zee lay-dee.'

The phone began to vibrate again. The girl reached over to answer it but the boy slapped her hand away. When at last the call was exhausted the boy snatched up the phone and tried dialling a long number. He listened for a dial tone and frowned. He tried again, pressing each button with slow deliberation. And again. His face became dangerously plastic as though he were on the point of tears. The very moment he stopped dialling the phone vibrated once more. He crawled out from under the piano and went over to a cloth-covered chair; he buried the phone – still alive – below a cushion. Before they left the children couldn't resist thumping the piano keys, thwang bang, a sonata for four elbows.

They hurried through the garden until they chanced upon two gardeners clipping a yew into a topiary whose form had yet to be revealed.

'Bonjour!' called the girl.

The gardeners downed their tools, curious and delighted. 'Bonjour!'

'Bonjour,' said the boy as he reached them. 'Je voudrais téléphoner,' he dialled an invisible phone, 'Australie.'

The gardeners tilted their heads and smiled benignly as though they couldn't quite understand his accent.

'Appeler Australie,' insisted the boy. He made another call on the imaginary phone.

'Téléphoner?' asked a gardener.

'Oui oui. Australie.' He tried again. 'Aus-stray-lie.'

The gardener shrugged and shook his head. 'Désolé.'

'Téléphoner.' The boy would not budge.

The other gardener spoke up. 'Assistance?'

'Oui oui.' The boy grew excited. 'Oui, assistance.'

'Assistance. Il faut appeler 4567.'

'4567.'

'C'est ça.'

'Merci-beaucoup-vous-êtes-très-gentil.' By rote. Mission accomplished. Away.

Back in their hidey-hole the boy tried once more to make a call. He allowed his accomplice to press the buttons 4, 5, 6, 7.

'Bonjour assistance?' said the boy. To the girl he reported, 'Recorded message. On hold.'

They waited. She rolled her eyes around and around.

'Oui.' He nudged the eye-roller and gave her the

thumbs up. 'Bonjour assistance.' He spoke slowly and clearly. 'Je voudrais téléphoner Australie.' There was a pause. 'Australie. Oui.' A little smile. He painstakingly wrote down a number on the notepad he had at the ready. 'Répétez lentement,' he said and checked over the figures.

'Merci-madame-vous-êtes-très-gentille.'

He dialled the number with that look of intense concentration often seen on children who are opening their birthday presents. Phone to ear, chin up. A frown – the unwanted gift. He tried again, pressing the buttons with more force as if this would aid the connection. Service denied.

'You broke it,' said the girl.

'It was already busted.'

There was nothing else for him to do but carefully rebury the phone underneath the cushion.

———◆———

When Marcus awoke the light was pinkening, so that it could have been dusk or dawn: penumbral. He had to check his watch to work out that night was falling. The woman was fast asleep on the sofa; near her mouth a little pool of drool had soaked into the cream silk upholstery. He stayed slumped in his chair as if his limbs had separated from his torso, only by a millimetre or two, so that he had to wait for fusion. At last – and all at once – he stood to his feet. Not wanting to disturb his sister he quietly took his leave but halfway across the room he froze and clasped a hand over his breast pocket, the way he would if he were having a heart attack. No phone. He patted down every pocket twice over. And a third time just to make sure. He lifted the cushions on his chair; he crawled around on the floor. For a long time he gripped the sides of his head, pressing his thumbs against his eyeballs.

Sophie did not wake when he stole into their room. She was curled on her side with a blood-stained pillow wedged between her thighs; the bundle lay beside her. Marcus began to rifle through his clothes, through the drawers. He worked methodically, in the practised man-ner of a spy who knows better than to make haste. Item by item he emptied out the baby-bag. No luck. The only sound was the soft purl of Sophie's breathing. He sighed, and at the end of the prolonged audible sigh was fortified. With great care he gathered up the bundle. Just then Sophie struggled to right herself.

'Marcus?'

'Hey.'

'I'm sorry, I'm so sorry. I just want – I wanted –' She stopped short, a sworn enemy of solace and reason.

'Me too.'

'I know.' Lowering her head.

He bowed down to kiss her cheek and then decamped to the kitchen.

———◆———

Later that evening the woman and the children were sitting with Grandmother upstairs in her suite. Grandmother and the girl were squeezed together on a small sofa, the boy was on the floor, the woman had her own chair: they were eating dinner in front of the TV. A bluish light jittered over their faces. The boy was concentrating on the program; his mother was not looking at the screen but was steadily watching her son's reactions. After a while he seemed to feel her eyes on his back and shuddered violently. He turned and glared at her – 'Stop it!' Unrepentant, she switched her attention to the TV. Every few minutes there came a burst of canned laughter but no-one watching laughed or even smiled. Grandmother forgot the program and observed the woman. It didn't take long for the woman to sense this and, turning to Grandmother, she conceded a small smile. They held one another's gaze and held and held. In her mother's face the woman saw all her mothers, countless faces of her mother, each fractionally different, one face streaming forward out of the next in the ghostly way of early stop-motion photography. Ghostly, milky with light.

'I like your hair like that,' Grandmother said quietly. 'It suits you.' She spoke for the sake of speaking.

After a pause the woman replied, 'Thank you.' There was no trace of formality in her voice. At that moment she became both very young and very old. Comforted, and with gratitude, mother and daughter pretended to take interest in the hullabaloo onscreen.

———◆———

During the night the girl started screaming. No crocodile tears, a real shrieking. The woman immediately awoke and sat up in her bed, listening. When the screaming did not abate she pulled on a dressing gown but found it too difficult to slip into with her cast and so wore it as a cape. She waited in the hallway outside the door to the children's room, the parquet cold beneath her feet. The girl's cries were growing increasingly ragged and breathless. The brass door handle was smooth and cool to the touch. At last a light came on under the door. The boy could be heard soothing his sister and soon the cries became sobs and swallowed gulps and then there was silence. Sophie came creeping down the hallway. The woman let her pass without comment.

In the kitchen the flowers from the funeral had been shoved head first into a garbage bin beside the walk-in fireplace. Those that didn't fit were piled against the bin as though votive offerings. Sophie sat alone at one end of the long wooden table. No lights had been turned on, there was only the faint glow of the moon. At her swollen breast she nursed a suction pump attached to a plastic bottle. She listened to the quiet hum of the battery-operated pump, the tick of the freezer, the occasional skitterings of night roaches. Outside the million-million green and growing things were absorbing oxygen. From time to time she winced and rearranged herself. Her eyes filled with tears. The level of her milk rose slowly.

—◆—

Ida wheeled Grandmother out to a commanding position in the middle of a lawn corridor which ran deep between two rows of steel-spun cypress. It was a day when the clouds were membrane-thin and very high, so high that it seemed the sky itself had recently expanded.

'To begin, Sophie,' said Grandmother, 'I have known you — for how long? Eight years. The day you were married to my son I was so proud, so happy, so proud. Your parents, bless them, if they could have been there I know they would have been proud too. And now – now I am very fond of you. It is a wonderful thing, to be married, to be welcomed into a new family. I was not born to this place. Ha – no, this,' she made a sweeping gesture, 'all this came to me by marriage. I married Maurice when I was just out of school – that young, yes. He was on vacation in New York and somehow my cousin made the introduction. I adored him. My husband . . . We had the children. First, Marcus. And then I was pregnant for a second time. For five months and . . . I lost it. What do they say – miscarried? As if it were as simple as misplacing. No, it was terrible. I know this – terrible.' She lowered her head. Looked up. 'A year later, we had Olivia. Our daughter. Our family. We were happy, Maurice and I. Ups and downs – yes, of course. He "chased skirt". I never said anything but I knew, there were signs: oh, long lunches, the usual. Once a friend even told me they'd seen him tête-à-tête in our favourite restaurant with . . . And there was an abortion.' The sign of the cross. 'Poor girl. But we weren't making love so how could I blame him? I let him run. There were the children to think of. And I loved him. For forty-two years I loved him and then one day, one afternoon, on a spring day not unlike today, he died. Dropped dead. Out of the blue. The heart. We buried him – over there.' She craned her neck and waved in the direction of the great oak. 'A week later my daughter left me. With no warning. First one, then the other – just like that. Well, it's true she fell in love with a pig. A pig. I'd tried everything to stop her but, of course – stone ears. Then one day: gone. It was as if she . . . vanished. I didn't hear from her for twelve years. Nothing. Not . . . nothing. And today she is home. Your child is with God. You have samples: there will be another. You must talk to your husband. You must bury this baby. In a short time no-one will speak of it. That is good. Things are not diminished by being left alone.'

When she had finished her speech Grandmother folded her hands in her lap, one over the other like a pair of gloves. Then the hands flew up as her audience suddenly departed.

Another day a light rain dimpled the lake. Marcus and the boy were nestled in the canoe, paddling in concert. The boy gazed across the water and asked, 'What's over there?'

'Over where?'

He pointed to the forest. 'There.'

'Forest. Miles and miles of forest. Hansel and Gretel forest. Sorry,' Marcus corrected himself, 'death-combat forest or whatever you prefer to call it. Full of wild boars. And then, the mountain. The village. Villages, I suppose.'

The boy just nodded. They continued to paddle, not bothered by the rain.

A short time later Marcus ventured, 'Andy, you haven't seen my phone have you?'

'What phone?'

'I lost it last week.' He faked a light-hearted sigh. 'Oh well. I'm sure it will just . . . turn up. Has this happened to you?' He placed his paddle across the canoe and turned to face the boy. 'Sometimes I just . . . lose things, they vanish. And then a few days later – voilà – they show up right there, under my nose. Strange. But what a relief.' He leant forward so that they were eye to eye. 'It's important to me to find that phone. A special friend of mine can only reach me on that number.' He sat back and resumed paddling. One stroke, two stroke.

Over his shoulder he added, 'You know, I'm always very grateful when things show up. Very grateful.'

——◆——

Days later an elaborate piece of garden furniture, a rattan throne, had been planted in the lawn corridor. The back of the throne was curved and high so that whoever sat in it was less mighty than the throne itself. The sun was at its peak, pinpointing every shadow. The priest solemnly approached the throne and after he had made himself comfortable he sat for a while without speaking. He raised the fingers of one hand.

'What God has given us, he can also take away,' he said, making a graceful arc with the hand. 'He is the beauty of childhood; He is the fullness of years. He knows that our love for Alice was not in vain.' He nodded his head. 'Blessed is He for the gift He gave us in her. We know that, in everything, He works for the good with those who love Him, who are called according to His purpose. We must give thanks to Him – not for taking our Alice from us – but for granting her a place with all the saints . . .'

There came a low hissing sound which gave him pause. He continued, 'We must bury Alice so that we can entrust her to God's eternal care.'

The guttural hissing grew louder and louder.

Discomfited, the priest raised his voice. 'So that she will live for ever in the joy and peace of His presence.'

Suddenly Sophie leapt to her feet and began attacking him. As she battered him with her fists he struggled to keep speaking.

'The Prophet Isaiah speaks of the time which is to come!' he shouted. 'Never again will there be in it an infant who lives but a few days! Or an old man who does not live out his years!! He who dies at a hundred will be thought a mere youth!! A youth!!! And he who fails to reach a hundred will be considered accursed!! Accursed!!'

She beat him to the ground.

———

The following morning Marcus took a load of his dirty shirts down to the laundry. It was a large room, almost a bunker, where solid metal troughs, hundreds of years old, ran alongside the very latest machines, the sort said to operate at the press of a button. The twins were packing away the gauzy muslin wraps, the baby-booties, all the small soft garments now redundant. One twin held up a little white jumpsuit and – she couldn't help herself – wiggled its weightless arm, space-walked it over to the cardboard box. Jumped it inside. And after that, each time they came across a jumpsuit the twins would make it animate. Marcus watched this pantomime from the doorway; he didn't try to stop them. And only when they accidentally caught a glimpse of him did he raise his voice, say, 'That's enough,' and he didn't say this out of a belated sense of propriety, or in anger, but rather in an attempt to stave off an apology. Alone, he finished the job with reverence.

The woman and the children, accompanied by Sophie and her bundle, were having an outdoor lunch below the great oak. Their picnic blanket was not far from the new little grave which had been covered with a square of bright green artificial grass. Neat heaps of dirt, some sprouting weeds, bordered this plastic grass. The woman was spooning a second helping of grated celeriac onto the side of the girl's china plate. There were no annoying flies; a pair of butterflies staggered overhead, conjoined at the abdomen. Ida stood nearby, ready to be summoned should the need arise. The boy was wandering around with an imaginary pistol in hand and when his mother called him over – 'Eat something' – he waved this pistol carelessly over each member of the picnic before training it on himself, pulling the trigger and blowing out his brains so that instead of simply sitting down he collapsed in a heap. It was such fun that he was resurrected and did it again: put the pistol to his temple and pulled the trigger, fell down. His sister and mother studiously ignored him. After a while he was resurrected once more. Sophie tired of the miracles and checked on her bundle in the white wicker bassinet; she lifted it out and brought it to her chest. The boy stared fixedly at Sophie until she looked down and noticed a little clump of fine dark hair sticking to her cream cashmere jumper. It didn't seem to bother her, this moulting, and she brushed off the hair as easily as she would breadcrumbs. The boy turned away and from the corner of his eye he caught sight of a deer which had wandered out from the line of trees, a fawn with spindle legs and oversized ears, a spotted coat and striped little tail. The first thing he did was lunge across and grab the girl, shove his hand over her mouth. He twisted her head in the direction of the newcomer. 'See, shh, be quiet.' When he felt her limp obeisance he released his grip and they all watched the fawn take uncertain steps on the thick soft lawn. For some unknown reason the animal turned to face them. The gaze held and held and in that gaze was wonder.

A strange thing happened: the bundle made a loud drawn-out squeak.

The fawn started and ambled away.

Sophie was fussing around; the others were appalled by the foul smell. The children held their noses.

———•—•———

This time it was Josette who lowered herself onto the rattan throne on the lawn, sitting straight and choosing not to use the backrest. She had come from the village and was wearing blue jeans and a cotton shirt, gold hoop earrings. Everything about her manner was clear and direct without being officious.

'Forgive me for intruding at this juncture,' she said. 'But as the representative of the State I must tell you that sufficient days have passed and you must now bury the baby or return the body to the morgue. These are the regulations.' She paused. 'The body is decomposing. The smell – the smell is a sign. Return the corpse to the earth. The skin will blister and fall away, the organs will bloat. Liquefy. Leak. Even the little ones leak. Millions of microbes inside the body will feast from within. And there may be coffin flies. It doesn't take long to be worn down to the bone.

The bones, they will outlast you. And one day they too will – crumble. Everything will be transformed: this is what happens. The earth is thriving. All you can do now is be gentle with yourself. The child's life is – done. The child is no longer suffering. She will remain in your thoughts. I do not believe in any soul, God is not the mystery, but I say – open your heart to those around you. Do not miss this chance. That's all.' She clasped her hands together. 'I hope we have reached an understanding.'

——◆——

One afternoon Marcus and the woman sat side by side in the summer pavilion; they were on the floor, backs straight against the wall, knees braced chinward. They had come here to seek respite from a burst of heavy rain but the rain had long since subsided. With the end of a twig the woman traced an invisible pattern into the stone.

'Every night I beg her to bury the baby,' said Marcus. 'And she always says it's not the right time. That's what she says, "Not yet, it's not the right time." '

The woman gave this some consideration. 'I'm sorry,'

she said softly. They looked into the garden. She added, 'Do you like the children? Are you fond of them?'

'They're wonderful,' he replied.

'Would you . . .' She made her pattern more intricate. Then she set down the twig and turned to face him. Her eyes were bright. 'Would you, and Sophie, like to . . . would you like to have them?'

'Have them?'

She stared at him. 'You could have them. Be their guardians.' Her voice came wholly from her chest, unexpectedly, the way it once did, only once, when she was a schoolgirl singing in a choir: unstoppered.

He recoiled a fraction. 'No, no, we couldn't,' he said, not meeting her gaze. Shook his head. 'No, Olivia, it's too great a gift. No, we couldn't accept.'

She studied him closely; he kept his eyes on the alps of his knees. She waited for a question or a word of comfort but neither was forthcoming. Eventually she turned away and looked once more into the garden, out beyond the lotus pond. Everything held steady there.

They continued to sit side by side in a hopeless silence.

'My murder,' she said. 'I volunteered and that is what is unbearable.'

The rain picked up, pelted the lawn. Her brother touched her shoulder to indicate he had heard her.

<hr />

At night the boy readied his escape. He had a small torch clenched between his teeth and was hard at work expertly organising provisions. His sister lay dead to the world. The contents to be packed were laid out on his bed: clothes, some small packages wrapped in foil, Marcus's phone. A kitchen knife. When he had finished his own pack he turned to the girl's. He heard a noise and froze – but it was only a mouse or a moth and the moment of danger was fleeting. Soon both packs were safely stashed behind the silk curtains that fell to the floor. He climbed onto his bed and touched Violet's breasts; he stood on tiptoes and gave the portrait a long fond kiss goodbye.

The woman made her own preparations. In the bathroom she stood naked before a mirror lit by a band of showgirl lightbulbs. Using her left hand she painstakingly tidied her eyebrows with the aid of a pair of tweezers. There was a glass ledge below the mirror which held a blue velvet make-up case and her bottle of heart-stopper, the digitalis. More than once she had trouble gripping the fine hairs, nipping the skin, and it took multiple attempts to pluck out each solitary hair. Not a muscle twitched though her eyes began to smart with tears. A rash of little red bumps formed under her eyebrows.

She studied the tip of her chin and plucked out two errant whiskers. She tilted back her head and searched for hairs growing in her nostrils. A hair sprouting from her right nipple came away.

She rubbed her face with a rose-scented moisturiser. She massaged the right side of her neck where the cast weighed heavy.

She sat on the edge of the bath and passed a soapy wet flannel over her calves. With a disposable razor she shaved her legs in long upward strokes, overlapping the strokes so as not to miss a hair. Despite her care she nicked herself on the right heel and her blood showed red and bright. She opened her legs and attended to her wiry bikini line. Hoisting the cast above her head she worked in the downy nook of her right underarm; it was hard going and she had to rest from time to time. The left underarm proved more difficult. At first she stretched her elbow up to the ceiling and tried to scoop down inside the nook with her left hand. When this didn't work she shifted the razor to the fingertips of her right hand and with great patience manoeuvred the razor-head from there.

After she had rinsed out the flannel she used it to wipe the soapy residue from her smooth soft skin. She looked at her fresh-shaven legs, the leg-bags, as if keenly aware of the minute difference between 'her' and 'there'. Back before the mirror she found that her reflection had remained faithful; she tested this by slowly pressing her lips together and seemed satisfied when the familiar stranger did the same.

The next morning Sophie was up early and walking in the garden, the bundle cradled in her arms. Her progress was slow, almost cautious; at each step she pressed down her heel and then unrolled the length of her foot in a wave-like movement that would not, could not, provoke any seismic shift. Behind her trailed a set of near-perfect foot-prints broken in the dew. A solitary blackbird sang out to confirm all existence and waited until there came an answering song.

The children were also awake, down by the water. Both were wearing their backpacks, the full load. The boy had rolled his jeans up over his knees and was standing at the lake's edge, sliding the canoe into the shallows. When he had it stable and buoyant he told his sister to climb inside. This she did, momentarily handing Pinky over for protection.

'Ida will know,' she said.

'Will not.' A gentle rebuff.

'Will so.' Said quietly. Head down, reclaiming her doll.

He scrambled into the canoe, catching his foot on the side and nearly stumbling headfirst over the prow. But he settled onto his captain's bench and, digging the paddle into the soft lake bed, he managed to turn the canoe so that they faced the forest, the mountain. This boy in a canoe on a lake before a forest below a mountain. Now begin the journey. He took a deep breath; he struck out. Splash, that paddle dragged through the water.

On land, standing behind a bank of blue hydrangeas, Sophie watched them go. Goodbye, goodbye: all the children go. When he had well and truly left the shore, the boy turned around for one last look over his shoulder, the gesture that marks the moment when leaving becomes arriving. He saw Sophie and she, likewise, saw him. After a moment she gave a little wave. Quickly he turned back toward the mountain. She watched the children go.

It was hard work, wielding the paddle. Steering was no easy business; the canoe tacked like a sailboat. Wobbled. A blister had already broken out on his palm.

'Andy?' said the girl, in her quietest voice.

He heard her but did not respond. He concentrated on paddling. One stroke, then the next. One stroke after the other. He fixed his eyes on his destination. At last he seemed to find a rhythm, left stroke, right stroke, and soon they were making a beeline toward the distant forest.

'Andy?' repeated the girl. He didn't answer: eyes on the prize, no time for distraction.

She tried again, louder this time. 'Andy?'

'What!'

Undertone. 'My feet are wet.'

Turning, he saw her feet resting in water. Somewhere, somehow, the canoe had sprung a leak. A leak. The boy did not panic; the canoe was taking on water; the boy remained calm. He would need to bail. To plug the leak. So he rustled under his bench and found a skeet of sorts, a small plastic bucket used to hold fish, and he leant over and started to empty out the lake. The girl lifted her feet, hugging her knees to her chest. Stay still. The lake sought its level. He bailed faster and faster. The girl wanted to help and so doing she accidentally knocked the paddle overboard. No, too late, it was out of his reach.

He waved his arms over his head, a wild semaphore. He called for help. The girl sat very still, was silent. Sophie was watching. He waved his arms again. He shouted. He could see her; she could see him. She did not move: Sophie was not coming to their aid. Now the world was undone.

And the world began again. This new boy seemed much like his predecessor – resolute and uncomplaining. So he bailed.

The woman approached the lake, taking her morning stroll. When she saw the listing canoe she began to run, to speed toward the shore, rushing blindly past the bank of hydrangeas, past Sophie, unseen though not hidden, right to the water's edge, the very precipice. Halt.

A small and puzzled frown crossed her brow. O. Her skin goose-pimpled, even her pupils dilated. Then, very slowly, as if working against a magnetic force, she lifted one foot and let fall her shoe. Let fall the other. She unpicked the knot of her sling. She shed her dress. Stepping forward, she incrementally immersed herself in the icy water, the lake close like a glove. Vile baptism.

She could hardly swim. Her cast was heavy and disabling. She stuck her head above the water and scrabbled like a dog. She kept going; she scrabbled and pawed and went under and came back up, she scrabbled and pawed. O it was icy cold. There were bottomless deeps beneath her. The canoe was taking on water; there were the children; she did not panic.

She pushed a clump of hair away from her mouth. Swallowed the lake, spat it out. She kept going. Distance played its favourite trick, egged her on.

A sharp pain in her right shoulder caused her to wince. It became difficult to breathe – how relentless, the breath. At last she had to stop. She turned onto her back, arms and legs outstretched, and opened her chest to the sky. The water filled her ears; her tiny earbones vibrated with the tripped-up thud of her heart. At that moment she was acutely alive. When her breath had settled she rolled over and resumed her swim.

She kept going. For hours, or was it for days? Time – there was no time, never had been – what a joke. She swam over the mountain. When the villagers saw her, this woman, scrabbling and pawing at the stony ground, filthy and near naked, with long strips of weed in her hair, her hands and knees bloodied, wearing a strange thick plaster on one arm, they gathered their children into their skirts and made them watch. See! The expression on the village children's faces was one of horrified wonder.

The canoe went under. When it happened, it happened quickly. The boy struggled to keep his sister afloat. The doll was lost. Neither child cried or even made a sound – as if a sound, a pip-squeak, could irrevocably tip the balance, send them down.

The woman scrabbled and pawed at the water. And though she scrabbled and pawed she wore on her face a small serene smile: O she was radiant. With her left hand she reached out to stabilise the girl, the three of them treading water. The boy she instructed in a kind and firm but breathless voice, 'Take off your pack.' After a moment's delay – he hesitated, she nodded in reassurance – he released the girl into his mother's care and laboured out of his backpack. Then between them they helped the girl. 'Now,' said the woman tenderly. 'Take her back.'

Once more he showed a look of doubt and when she repeated herself, again with great tenderness, he pursed his mouth and blinked rapidly. 'It's okay,' she said. 'Go on.' He told the girl to lie on her back, which she did without protest, and slipped his arm under her neck in order to support her head. The girl played dead. He started to tow her and had not gone far before he looked back over his shoulder. His mother was treading water; she lifted her hand and waved him toward the shore.

She did not begin the return journey. Instead she jelly-fished: she took a great gulp of air and, belling her back and letting her arms fall loose, submerging her face in the water, she hung suspended. Each time she could no longer hold her breath she let out a stream of bubbles before briefly lifting her head, taking another great gulp and then returning to the water. She floated. She appeared – she was – a simple life-form, with no mind other than mind-through-body, a nerve net, and with each new breath, each new shocking breath, she was reborn; it would take an aeon for her to be human. The lake let her be.

When the boy reached the shore he saw to it that his sister was safe. She sat very quietly on the sand, though she couldn't stop her teeth from chattering. He stood beside her, heaving and gasping; he had his hands on his hips and there were little shadows in the hollows beneath his bony shoulderblades. As soon as he had modulated his breath he re-entered the water.

In the middle of the lake he waited for the woman to resurface. He made small shallow circles in the water to better help him stay in place. It seemed she could hold her breath for ever. At last she came up for air. There he was: her boy. They weren't far from one another, a metre or so, and there was a long silence until the boy said – or implored – 'Please. Come on.'

She closed her eyes, turned onto her side. He towed her in. More than once he dunked his heavy load. On the sand she crouched on all fours and pitched and gagged. The boy lay flat on his back looking up at the sky; the girl, shivering, watched over him. Soon after the commotion the lake was distilled; it disdained secrets, held nothing.

When she had recovered the woman bunched her belongings to her chest and proceeded toward the house with small measured steps. The children followed at a distance, hand in hand, knobbled by the cold. She stopped when she caught sight of Sophie: Sophie, who had not moved an inch from her observation post, who had not relinquished her bundle. At first the woman glanced at her with a kind of weary solidarity, a war widow's glance, but sensing a defiance, some sort of refusal, the woman almost did a double take; she stared at Sophie for a long time. Sophie stood unrepentant. The children joined their mother, dragged her away.

Ida and the twins were busy fixing breakfast in the kitchen. One twin was watching over the pop-up toaster, the other was ladling boiled eggs out of a saucepan. Ida was rummaging around in the pantry looking for a replacement pot of raspberry jam. When the sodden bedraggled trio appeared in the doorway the twins were quick to rush to their assistance. Ida, leaving the pantry, gasped and grew pale.

'We had an accident,' said the woman.

Ida got on her knees before the girl. 'There, there, my little one. My darling.'

The girl gave her the bare and crestfallen look of the betrayed. 'Pinky's gone.'

'No, my darling, no no,' said Ida. 'Come here, come here little one.' She hugged her close.

Marcus entered the fray. He cast an anxious glance around the room.

'She's by the lake,' said the woman coldly.

He hurriedly excused himself, departed.

———

That night the woman put the children to bed. First she tucked in the boy as best she could with one hand, kissed him on the forehead. The girl she tucked in too. They lay perfectly still and straight. She made sure they both had a glass of water beside their beds. Standing by the light switch she said, 'Goodnight, darlings. Ni-night.' It was dark, they listened to her footsteps. As soon as it was safe the boy reached over and switched on his lamp. The girl pushed back her sheets and changed beds, squirmed in beside him. Stay close. The lamp went off and it was dark again.

The woman stood by the window, the curtains were open and she beheld a small herd of deer that had gathered on the lawn, fearlessly close to the château; the deer were standing and staring, their eyes glinted, reflecting the light from her room. A berserk star caught her attention: it might have been a plane.

——•——

At first light the sky turned a deep orange, a smoky grey, a tallow white, and then grey once more until – annealed – the day broke powdery blue. A long dark scratch against the sky turned to cloudbank. The woman was bent low pulling the artificial grass off the small grave beside the headstone. She was dressed in a pearl-grey tweed suit, stockings and heels. Her broken arm was hidden in a blue silk sling. And she had fixed her hair, a loose chignon, and had gone to the trouble of putting on make-up. To her left was the tiny walnut casket that she had dragged over from the house. First she removed the square of grass, kicking it into a heap; then she manoeuvred the casket as close as she could to the earthen maw. She worked methodically, not with stealth but with blatant purpose.

On the way back to the house she made a detour via the rose garden. Without thought for the look of the plants she took her scissors to the blooms. One by one the roses fell to the ground and when she had a sufficient number, fifteen or so, she pocketed the scissors and collected the stems with her left hand, thorns and all.

She marched into the kitchen, ignoring Ida, ignoring the twins, and dumped the roses on the wooden table. She headed hellbent toward the freezer and – stunned – they did not try to stop her. The freezer, the top compartment lined in pink satin, was empty save for a little lace-trimmed pillow. Slightly disconcerted, she turned to leave but on afterthought turned back to double-check its silver pair, the refrigerator. Every shelf was crammed with food. No matter; she slammed the door shut and, brushing past the twins – 'Excuse me' – strode away.

'Get up! Wake up!' She broke into the children's room. 'Lucy! Andrew!' she yelled. 'Get dressed! Hurry! Get up!'

The children scrambled to attention. She threw open the left curtain. On hands and knees she rooted through the clothes heaped carelessly on the floor until she found the outfits they had worn at the funeral, the suit and the black velvet dress, and she tossed these, garment by garment, onto the girl's bed. After swapping glances with one another the children hurried to unbutton their pyjamas.

She buzzed insistently on the intercom outside Grandmother's suite. Five times. Six times. One uninterrupted demand until the door could be heard to click. Stormed through the rooms, called out, 'Wake up! Get dressed! Hurry!'

Grandmother had pulled up the bedsheet to a level just below her eyes, timorous. The woman ripped it away. She grabbed Grandmother's shoulder, skin and bone, and gave her a strong shake. 'Get ready!'

Ida rushed in and with a placatory gesture – gently cupping the woman's elbow – she insinuated herself between Grandmother and assailant. The woman released her grip and waited hand on hip as Grandmother clambered out of bed. Ida helped her to her feet and while Grandmother wasn't looking, searching for her slippers under the bed, she nodded to the woman in tacit approval.

Marcus, all bleary-eyed and wearing a clumsily tied dressing gown, slumbered down the hallway. He lifted his shoulders in an open-palmed shrug that said, What's going on?

'Sophie is ready,' said the woman.

'She's ready? Now?'

'Yes. Now.' Curt.

Without losing momentum she sidestepped around him and marched toward his room. After a moment he followed.

The room was empty: no Sophie. Nowhere, not there. She opened the door of a neighbouring room. A draught of air set an intricate kiddy-mobile turning and tinkling. Here was a nursery, with a wooden cot and a rocking-horse, a large doll's house. The walls and ceiling were painted fingernail-pink and sprinkled with silver stars. No Sophie.

And the next room – she gripped the door handle like she would grip at the rung of a ladder, then wrenched it down. No Sophie. The full length of the hallway: door open, door closed, door open, door closed, door open . . . unstoppable. Every room was empty.

She scuttled down the central staircase, weightless, her left hand lightly passing over the banister. Looking straight ahead, the exact breadth and depth of each stair an engrained bodily knowledge. In the entrance hall she hesitated a moment and then turned sharp left into the drawing room, yanking open the door. Empty, all the furniture shrouded. She went over to the windows and banged behind the curtains, sniffed and sniffed. Nothing there. Halfway across the room she stopped and scratched furiously in the small space between her skin and her cast. Then she turned on her heels, marched back to the entrance hall and crossed into the salon whose walls were spiked with antlers. Sophie was wearing her coffee-silk nightgown and was sitting peaceably on a chaise longue. The white wicker bassinet rested within arm's reach on a low table. She did not seem surprised by the intrusion, not in the slightest; the impression she gave was that nothing whatsoever was amiss. Without pause the woman walked over to the table until she and Sophie were equidistant from the bassinet. There they held one another's gaze. Very slowly the woman leant forward, reaching out her left hand toward the bassinet, and Sophie mirrored this movement, reaching at the same pace – but not grabbing, not snatching – until their fingertips were almost touching. And the woman, unwavering, settled her hand onto the wicker bands, closed her fist. It was heavy, the bassinet. She carried it away.

———

Once more they encircled the open grave. The woman was there, the bassinet by her feet; the children were dressed in their finest. Grandmother sat very straight in her wheelchair, tended by Ida and the twins. Two solemn gardeners were armed with shovels. Sophie, still in her nightgown, was at the head of the grave and Marcus stood beside her.

The woman transferred the bundle from the bassinet to the casket. Afterwards there was a long pause until Marcus assumed the lead and, kneeling down, lay a rose beside the corpse. At his encouragement Sophie did the same. Grandmother was next, Ida wheeled her forward. The girl took a deep breath and quickly had her turn, followed by the woman. And the boy was last. He balled his hand over the head of the rose so that only the stem was protruding. They waited. The girl, helpful, pointed her finger over and over toward the ground. His mother nodded at him as if to say, Continue. Eventually he obeyed. Arching up he saw that Sophie had also broken out of their circle and was now staring at him. She tried to touch his shoulder but he shrugged her off. Her fledgling smile was sad and tender and asked of him forgiveness. The boy was mountain and lake. Marcus drew her back.

The gardeners lowered the casket into the grave. They set about with their shovels, scattering dirt on wood. Ida gave a loud sigh of relief.

In the garden the clipped topiaries, the long rows of cypress, the rose beds, the lotus, the elms, the poplars, the great oak, each nipped blade of grass – all were animate, transforming sunlight, and the woman, breathing in, breathing out, sensed this, felt this silent and constant becoming, was a part of it, and this burgeoning feeling, gentle and immanent, so long dormant, spilled from behind her sternum and into her throat, it filled the space behind her mouth, behind her nose until – practised – she did not so much cut it off or snuff it out as simply let it pass. All things can be refused. The next moment she turned toward her son. *My child.* He was ancient and implacable, a boy most beautiful. But no boy is mountain and lake and knowing this – knowing that mountain is rock and lake is water, that even rock sheds fine grains and water shapeshifts, knowing it impossible to be rock or water, and knowing the disappointments she had visited upon herself – she made a wish for him. *Hold, hold.*

Acknowledgements

Australia Council for the Arts; The Authors' Foundation (UK); The Marten Bequest Travelling Scholarships; Rolex Mentor and Protégé Arts Initiative; University of Adelaide.